Praise for ANGEL LOST...

"A pervert threatens women joggers on the beach, a robber threatens wealthy homes on the bluff, and an angel watches over the townspeople from a downtown window. F. M. Meredith's latest Rocky Bluff P. D. novel is a gentle human drama about loneliness and change, through which the reader is pulled, page after page, by an assortment of compelling criminal curiosities." – C. N. Nevets is an author of psychological suspense.

ANGEL LOST is the kind of story that hooks the reader's curiosity from the first paragraph. It is another standalone in the Rocky Bluff P.D. crime series from F. M. Meredith, a pen name for Marilyn Meredith, the prolific writer who, among other her other works, also writes the popular Tempe Crabtree mysteries. ANGEL LOST is an engrossing story of small town police officers, their lives, professional and personal, and the inevitable interactions that their police work, plus living in a small town, provides them. Words and deeds travel fast in these communities and there are few secrets kept intact in Rocky Bluff. The reader is placed among these insiders hearing the same whispers and gossip.

This is a suspenseful story with a bit of religious mysticism thrown into the mix—just enough to broaden the plot and provide added depth to the characterizations. It should appeal to a wide range of readers and will provide a satisfying reading experience thanks to the author's smooth and fluid writing style – Kit Sloane, author of *The Magicians*, the latest in the Margot & Max Mystery series.

In ANGEL LOST, author Marilyn Meredith has created a thrilling adventure that weaves together the lives of several point-of-view police officers, with Officer Stacy Wilbur and Detective Doug Milligan in starring roles. I truly, truly, TRULY loved every minute of this terrific story! Read it yourself and find out why. – Radine Trees Nehring, Author of the Carrie McCrite and Henry King "To Die For" mystery series.

F.M. Meredith has another hit on her hands with her latest installment of the Rocky Bluff P.D. series. A fast-moving mystery full of suspense, well-developed characters and realistic interpersonal relationships, Angel Lost wants for nothing. Meredith weaves a compelling story that keeps you guessing with a satisfying ending guaranteed to please even the most discerning mystery lover. Impossible to put down, Angel Lost is the first must-read of the year. – Holli Castillo, author of *Gumbo Justice.*

Angel Lost is the seventh in F. M. Meredith's Rocky Bluff Police Department series, and fans of this series will be delighted to learn that it delivers everything we have come to expect in these books – characters that feel like neighbors and a handful and a half of subplots all neatly woven together. Detective Doug Milligan is set to marry Officer Stacey Wilbur. As their wedding day approaches he is unhappy about not getting to spend much time with her but even more unhappy about her assignment to jog the beach in hopes of catching a pervert who has been exposing himself to women. Abel Navarro's mother is showing signs of Alzheimer's, the new transfer from the LAPD has a problem that won't be solved merely by transferring to a small town, and a reflection on a plate glass window downtown is seen by some as a sign from God because it appears to be an angel. Others see it as just a quirky reflection. The Rocky Bluff PD sees it as a distraction because of the crowds that gather each night to see it. Just as these things seem to be coming to a head, a serial kidnapper and perhaps murderer who has been working his way south from Oregon shows up. Meredith wraps everything up in a most satisfactory fashion. These books are a sort of cross between *The Waltons* and *Hill Street Blues*, and I hope there are many more to come. – J. Mike Orenduff, The Pot Thief mysteries.

ANGEL LOST

By F. M. Meredith

Oak Tree Press Taylorville, IL

Oak Tree Press

Oak Tree Press books may be purchased for educational, business or sales promotional purposes. Contact Publisher for quantity discounts.

First Edition, February 2011
Cover by MickADesign.com
Interior Design by Linda W. Rigsbee

ISBN 978-1-61009-005-6
LCCN 2011921065

Dedicated to Keith Bettinger who helped me a lot with one of my characters and to the Public Safety Writers Association that keeps me connected to people in law enforcement despite the fact they sometimes shudder at what I've written.

Disclaimer: This is what I always tell people when I give talks about the Rocky Bluff P.D. crime series:

"I'm writing fiction. It's my police department so I can do it anyway I want."

And once again to my critique group that is absolutely invaluable: thank you Shirley, Jann, Kristi and Brent.

Last but not least, to daughter Dana Van Scoy who made some great suggestions about the book.

■

CHAPTER 1

"OFFICER WILBUR, ARE you listening?" Detective Doug Milligan fixed his blue eyes on Stacey.

She squirmed in her seat and felt the heat rise up her neck to her cheeks. The honest answer was "no" because she'd been thinking about plans for their coming wedding, certainly not the topic being discussed at the shift change briefing. She quickly back-tracked to what she last remembered—the man who exposed himself to female joggers on the beach. Since she figured they might have gone onto another subject without her realizing, she decided to be honest. "Sorry."

The others in the room stared at her. Doug's partner, the nearly bald Frank Marshall had a bemused expression on his face. He unwrapped a stick of gum, folded it, and put it in his mouth. Chewing gum had replaced a smoking habit. He winked at her.

Stacey figured he guessed what she'd been thinking about. Having everyone speculating about her private life had been one of the reasons Stacey vowed never to date anyone on the Rocky Bluff P.D.—a vow she'd broken when she and Doug had been attracted to one another.

Handsome Ryan Strickland, the public relations officer for Rocky Bluff P.D., reached over and patted her hand. "We know you have more important things on your mind with your wedding less than a week away—but since there's a pervert who decided to make jogging on the beach an unpleasant experience for females, maybe you ought to pay attention, since it does fall under your job description."

Shrugging and grinning, Stacey said, "What can I say? You're absolutely right, my mind was elsewhere. Sorry. I'm listening now, but I did hear most of it." She absently caressed the teardrop diamond in her engagement ring.

The group around her murmured and she heard a few chuckles. In attendance besides Doug, Frank and Ryan, were most of the patrol officers on the daytime shift, including Gordon Butler. Sergeant Abel Navarro and the men who worked the evening hours were still there too.

Stacey was thankful Chief McKenzie was absent. He might regret making her head of the vice team—a team that so far consisted only of her.

"We've had our third complaint in the last two weeks about a man on the beach exposing himself to unsuspecting female joggers." Doug glanced at the notes on his desk. "It's probable that the same thing has happened to others, but they haven't bothered to report it."

He looked so much younger since he'd shaved his mustache. Stacey remembered when she first came on the department almost every officer had a mustache; now most were clean-shaven. Without the mustache, Doug's dimples were even more prominent. She shook her head. Time to pay attention and stop admiring her future husband.

Doug continued. "This guy is a real scumbag. He usually fondles himself and talks nasty to the victims. None of them could remember exactly what he said because they immediately ran away. The last young woman, a Claudine Graham, reported that the man started following her. I think this pervert is getting braver and may attack a woman."

"Is there a pattern? Does he do this at any particular time?" Stacey asked. "Do you have an accurate description?"

"That's what I was talking about when you spaced out on us." Doug's grin softened the sting of his words. "This has always happened early in the morning, between 6:30 and 8 a.m. Seems all three victims like to jog before going to work. Yes, we do have a description, a white male, anywhere from late twenties to early forties, close to six foot tall and around 200 pounds. Wears a watch cap so don't know his hair color."

"What do you want to do about the suspect? Put someone on beach patrol? Maybe I could start jogging during that time period and catch the pervert in the act." Stacey knew if anyone but Doug was in charge he would jump at the chance to use her as a decoy. She could tell by Doug's hesitation that he wasn't thrilled by the idea.

Abel Navarro spoke. "That's a great idea, Wilbur."

"I suppose it is," Doug smoothed back his dark hair and tapped on the desk with his pen. "We'll provide you with back-up."

"Probably won't be necessary. It's cool in the morning. I can carry my gun and cuffs in my jacket." Though Stacey was small, five foot four and one-hundred five pounds, people still talked about the time she took down a nearly three-hundred pound would-be bank robber. Luck had played a big part in the arrest, plus the suspect had been shocked by a petite female having the guts to confront him. All the men in the bank, including the security guard, had cowered. No matter, the incident had given her a status in the department she was quite happy to have.

"At least call in before you head out. That way, a unit can be close by if the suspect crosses your path." The scowl on Doug's face made it obvious he wasn't pleased with the idea.

One of the uniformed officers, a recent transfer from LAPD, raised his hand. Stacey had to think a moment to remember his name. Vaughn Aragon, that was it. She didn't know much about him except that he'd told a couple of guys that he wanted to get away from big city crime. Sandy-haired and lightly-freckled, he wasn't as short as Abel Navarro, but was at least three inches under six-foot. She guessed he was at least thirty, maybe older. She'd heard he was recently divorced. Although he didn't look Hispanic, he could speak Spanish, the main reason he'd been hired.

When he was acknowledged by Doug, Aragon said, "I worked a similar case in L.A. at Venice beach."

Doug nodded. "Why don't you and Wilbur work on this together?"

Swell, she was going to be saddled with someone she didn't even know. Aragon turned in his seat and grinned. Without any enthusiasm, she smiled back.

The meeting continued as a rash of burglaries in the wealthiest part of Rocky Bluff were discussed. In each case, the thief had found easy access to the expensive homes. Possibly the owners felt unwisely secure because of the location.

Some of the oddest happenings of the day were also brought up, from the report of a poisoned squirrel dying on a front lawn, two peacocks strutting down a residential street interfering with traffic, and a woman who thought her boyfriend was missing but was found asleep in their bed.

When the meeting was over and those on the late shift headed toward their police units, Aragon approached Stacey. "How should we go about this?" He seemed nervous.

Stacey motioned to the chair near hers. "Why don't you tell me how the similar case you were on was handled?"

He turned the chair around and straddled it. "It was a lot like this one. Pervert approached from the opposite direction on the beach like he was taking an early morning stroll. When he neared the female jogger, he'd open his coat and grab himself. Usually made some kind of nasty suggestions, though most of his victims didn't hang around long enough to hear what he said."

"Did your guy ever try to attack any of these women?"

"No, we caught him right away."

"How did you do it?"

"Pretty much like you suggested. One of the female cops jogged along the same stretch of beach and the very first time she did it, the guy approached her. I'd been sitting farther up the beach watching with binoculars. She exchanged words with him and I got there in time to help with the arrest."

Stacey nodded. "Hopefully, it'll go that way for us too. Tomorrow's my day off and I have too much to do to give it up."

"Stuff for the big wedding day, right?" Aragon displayed his full set of slightly crooked teeth in an enormous grin.

She decided to ignore his question. He didn't know her well enough to tease her, but the police department was like a small town, everyone liked to gossip. Right now, her upcoming wedding to Doug was the hottest topic. Too bad there wasn't a gruesome murder to grab everyone's interest. She shook her head. She couldn't believe such a thought popped into her mind.

"We'll start day after tomorrow. Meet me at the condemned pier at seven a.m. I'll point out the places where each victim had her encounter with this jerk. That should help us choose the best spot for you to watch while I jog. If nothing else, I'll get some exercise."

■

Doug caught up with Stacey in the parking lot. "How about coming back to the house for awhile?"

Stacey grinned at him. "As much as I'd like to, I think I better get home. I've got a lot to do tomorrow."

"I know, but do you have time for a cup of coffee at least? We could stop at the diner. I wanted to talk to you about this pervert. I'm not so sure I want you to be a decoy."

"Okay. A cup of coffee."

Though Doug suggested she ride with him, she declined. Driving her yellow VW, she followed his black SUV. When they'd met, Doug drove a red vintage MG he'd restored. The SUV didn't seem like the right vehicle for him. Unfortunately, his pride and joy had been sunk in a lagoon by a suspect. Though it had been fully insured, he'd replaced it with the SUV, reasoning it was more suitable for a family man. Perhaps he was right as there was plenty of room, even for the times his two children might visit.

They parked in front of the diner located on Valley Boulevard, the main street of Rocky Bluff. A favorite with cops and civilians alike, the diner, aptly called The Gathering Place, stayed open twenty-four hours a day, seven days a week. According to the newspaper clipping framed on the wall, the establishment opened its doors in 1939. It was laid out like many diners of an older era, with a counter down one side and booths on the other. Through the years, each new owner had rejuvenated it with a paint job, new curtains and decorations. Though everything was fresh and clean, the latest version reflected an earlier time with blue and white gingham curtains and shelves filled with old-fashioned kitchen equipment like old toasters, mixers, bread boxes and cheese graters. The waitresses wore blue and white gingham aprons, though underneath most wore white blouses and dark slacks.

Once Doug and Stacey settled in their favorite booth at the back of the room, with steaming cups of coffee in front of them, she said, "Don't say anything about the pervert on the beach. It's my job to take care of these kinds of cases now."

Reaching across the blue and white speckled Formica table-top, Doug took one of her hands. "That's not what's bothering me. We really don't know much about this new guy, Aragon. I'd be much happier if someone else was going to back you up."

"Like who? Gordon?" Stacey's blue eyes twinkled.

"No, as much as I like Butler, he'd probably botch the whole thing."

"Sounds like Aragon has a lot more experience than Gordon. I really don't see how anything can go wrong."

"Something can always go wrong."

Nodding, Stacey squeezed his hand. "Yes, and it can go wrong with weddings too. That's why I have to go home early tonight and really concentrate on everything that I still have to do. Tomorrow is going to be a busy day."

Doug sipped some coffee. He'd be so happy when he and Stacey were finally married and she and her son Davey lived with him. "Sometimes I wish I hadn't agreed to a big wedding."

She shook her head. "You didn't and we aren't having one. This is a small ceremony in the church with only our relatives and close friends."

"Close friends meaning all the police officers who don't have to work along with their wives and kids."

"And my mom and dad and Davey."

"Of course." He sipped his coffee and swallowed hard. "It just seems the plans keep expanding."

Stacey raised her eyebrows and tipped her head. "Sounds like you're getting nervous. You aren't having second thoughts, are you?"

"Absolutely not. I can hardly wait." They'd already picked out matching wedding rings and gotten their marriage license. He wished they could have a simple ceremony at the court house, but Stacey and her parents were adamant that their wedding be performed by their minister and in the church.

He studied Stacey. Her short honey-colored hair curled slightly around her elfin face that was nearly devoid of make-up. She was so different than his first wife. Though beautiful, Kerrie couldn't stand the fact that he was a policeman. When one of their best friends was killed on the job, that was the end of the marriage. Stacey filled the void left by his divorce. Of course he missed his kids, but Stacey's six-year-old son, Davey, helped ease that pain. He was eager to be a full-time father again.

She frowned. "That's good because I've spent a lot of time and money trying to make everything perfect." When she broke into giggles, Doug knew she was teasing.

"I thought we weren't planning anything extravagant." Every time she started talking about what she was doing, it made him nervous. No doubt their ideas of a small wedding weren't the same. He hadn't been asked to foot the bill for anything and, so far, had only paid for the rings. It wasn't the expense that was bothering him. He'd already experienced one big wedding and the outcome wasn't good. He was hoping a much smaller event and their love would result in a lasting commitment.

"Trust me, sweetheart." A smile lingered on her full lips. "It will be far from extravagant, but I do want it to be nice. My plan is to make our special day something we'll both remember."

■

Abel thought about what went down at home before he'd left for work.

Before his wife, Maria, even kissed him goodbye, her dark eyes flashed as she said. "I don't want you to leave Lupita with your mom any more."

She had never gotten along with Abel's mother, but this was the first time Maria had been so adamant about the babysitting problem. He worked the four to midnight shift in order to care for their daughter in the daytime while Maria worked as a nurse at the local hospital.

"You know I don't do it that much. I just dropped her off for a couple of hours today so I could take care of errands. It's such a pain putting Lupita in the car seat and then taking her out again every place I have to stop."

"Something's very wrong with your mother, Abel. I know that you or your brothers don't notice, but she's been getting worse lately."

At first Abel thought Maria was being petty, but when he noticed how intense she looked, he asked, "What do you mean? I haven't noticed anything different." But when he thought about it, there was something a bit off about the way his mom was acting lately.

"For one thing, she's started being nice to me."

Abel grinned. "Isn't that good? Maybe she just decided to try and get along with you." That would certainly be a nice change. His mother had a way of saying things, especially to her daughters-in-law, that on the surface were okay, but carried a hidden sting.

"No, sweetheart, it's more than that. Haven't you noticed the house isn't quite as neat as it used to be? How she keeps telling the same stories over and over? Sometimes she asks the same question right after you answered."

He had observed some of those things. "But isn't that just part of getting older?"

"Your brothers' wives have noticed too. We've been talking about what's going on among ourselves. The worst that's happened that I know about, is that she got lost on her way to the dentist. She called Veronica to ask how to get there." Veronica was his brother Juan's wife.

"That could happen to anyone." Even though he defended his mother's action, a tiny worm of worry squirmed in Abel's brain.

"Think about it. Your mother has been going to the same dentist for years."

Abel sighed. "What do you think is wrong with her?"

Maria's voice softened. "I know you don't want to hear this, Abel, but I'm guessing some form of dementia. The personality change, getting lost, not being able to do all the things she usually did so easily. She might even have Alzheimer's."

"Oh, God. How can you be sure that's what's wrong?" His mother was the strong one in the family. She'd never had any major illness or been in the hospital except when she gave birth to her sons.

"I think you boys need to talk with your father. At the very least, your mom needs a good physical. There are so many new medicines on the market for Alzheimer's now, but they work best when they're started at the onset of the disease."

"My dad isn't going to believe anything's wrong with mom." His parents had been married for forty-eight years and as far as his father was concerned his wife was about as close to perfect as anyone could get. No one could be critical of his wife within his hearing without being chastised.

"You might be surprised. He's living with her. He's bound to have noticed the changes but is afraid to tell anyone."

"I'll give my brothers a call and see what they say."

"Don't wait too long." Maria's voice changed back into her take charge nurse mode. "And in the meantime, don't leave Lupita with her."

"You can't deprive my mom of seeing our daughter. She loves her grand-kids, you know that."

"I didn't say she couldn't see Lupita, I just don't want her taking care of her. It's not safe for Lupita."

Abel wasn't sure he accepted his wife's diagnosis of his mother's problem. It couldn't be as bad as Maria described. Everyone changed as they got older. His father certainly wasn't as spry as he once was and now that he was retired he spent what seemed like an excessive amount of time fiddling with his Koi fish and their pond. "Aye, one more thing to worry about," he muttered when he went out the door.

■

Felix Zachary, the only black officer on the Rocky Bluff P.D., had a bad feeling in his gut about the newest addition to the Department, Vaughn Aragon. He'd partnered with Aragon his first two weeks on patrol. The guy never looked like he had enough sleep and acted jittery.

It got on Felix's nerves how Aragon kept saying, "Wow, this is great, just like I was hoping. Hardly any rough stuff. You can't believe how much easier it is here, just handing out traffic tickets and investigating burglaries. All I did in L.A. was clean-up after gang shootings and grisly murders. It gets to you after awhile."

Felix tried to tell him that Rocky Bluff had its share of murders and violence too, but not as many since they were a lot smaller than Los Angeles.

Aragon didn't agree. "All you've got around here is petty crime. You don't know what it's like to have to shoot some kid."

Felix did know what it was like. He'd shot a young man he and several other officers had been pursuing. Shots were fired. Felix was the first to catch up with the suspect. After all the previous shooting, when the suspect reached into his dungarees, Felix figured the guy was going after a weapon and shot him. Later, after the suspect died, Felix learned there was no weapon and the first shots he'd heard had been one of the other officer's gun going off accidentally. Felix was suspended with pay until a full investigation cleared him, but he'd lost his bid on becoming sergeant because of the incident. Even worse was the mental anguish that lasted for months after he'd killed the unarmed suspect, depressing him to the point of considering suicide.

Mandatory counseling had helped, but his wife's love and faith had finally pulled him out of the pit.

Something about this new Aragon guy reminded Felix of himself during his darkest hours. He was sure Chief McKenzie had done a thorough check prior to accepting the man's lateral transfer. Even though there was no evidence to support Felix's feelings, something about Aragon nagged at Felix.

■

Vaughn Aragon hoped working with the cute female officer trying to catch the pervert bothering female joggers would help his fellow cops accept him. So far he hadn't even been able to find a drinking buddy. He didn't believe all these guys were teetotalers, although most of them seemed to be married, or about to be. Marriage hadn't kept him from going to the local cop hangout after a shift, one of the excuses his ex used for leaving him.

He got bad vibes from the black dude, Zachary. Something about him rubbed Vaughn the wrong way. He couldn't put his finger on it. Zachary treated him okay when they were on duty together, but it was like he was trying to worm his way inside his soul. He asked far too many questions, questions Vaughn wasn't about to answer.

The friendliest of his new co-workers was Gordon Butler, a baby-faced, pink-cheeked guy with three years under his belt, but who still had the obnoxious enthusiasm of a rookie.

After settling on a time to meet with Stacey Wilbur, Vaughn hurried after Butler. In the parking lot, he hollered, "Hey, Butler, wait up."

Butler turned, but a slight frown marred his usually smooth forehead. "What can I do for you?"

"Wondered if you'd show me where the guys hang out after a shift? Maybe have a beer with me. Make the new guy feel welcome."

Butler blinked a few times. "I don't usually go anywhere but home after work, not even sure there is a hangout." His cheeks turned a brighter pink. "But sure, I'll have a beer with you. A couple of times I went with Doug, that's Detective Milligan, to a place called The Library where he and a bunch of the guys used to go sometimes." He pointed to a non-descript sedan. "My car is that black Toyota over there."

"Sounds good. I'll follow you."

Vaughn trailed after Butler in his yellow and black Mini Cooper, the only thing he had left after the divorce. The Mini Cooper had been his wife's, not really his choice of vehicle, but she'd been awarded his 1987 Mustang in the divorce settlement because he still owed on the Mini-Cooper. Just one more way she took him to the cleaners.

Butler drove his Toyota sedan like an old lady, at least two miles under the speed limit. It made Vaughn nuts. Fortunately, Butler only went about three miles before he turned into the parking lot of a store-front bar. Not too promising—even less so when they went inside.

It wasn't smoky. No bars in California were smoky anymore because smoking in a public place was against the law. It wasn't even particularly dark inside, mainly because of the two flat screen TVs near the ceiling displaying the latest games. No one seemed to be watching. A few older guys nursing drinks sat at the bar that ran the length of the room having what seemed to be an important conversation. Might've been retired cops, Vaughn couldn't be sure.

Butler chose a round table with a glass top near one corner of the room. Under the glass were several patches from different departments. Guess this was a cop bar after all. Once they were seated, a middle-aged waitress approached, wearing a black short skirt that struck her mid-thigh. Her skinny legs ended in sensible flat sandals. She wore a T-shirt with an embroidered logo, *The Library* scrawled across the spines of several books. A name plate pinned to her collar identified her as Mindy. Her dyed blonde hair was pulled back into a ponytail with several wisps stringing down around her angular face.

"Hey, Butler, isn't it? Haven't seen you for awhile, or your buddy Milligan. Heard a rumor that he's getting married." She put a bowl of mixed nuts on the table.

"It's true, he's marrying Stacey Wilbur."

"Good for him. I always liked Officer Wilbur. She only came in here once or twice, but I could tell she had lots of spunk. Tell him Mindy says congratulations."

"Will do."

"What can I get for you two?"

"A Bud Lite for me." Butler gestured toward Vaughn. "This is Aragon, transferred from LAPD."

"I'll have a Coors in a bottle. Pleased to meet you, Mindy."

Mindy smiled, displaying a chipped front tooth. "Be back in a minute."

"So what's the skinny on Detective Milligan. Sounds like he used to hang out here."

"His wife left him because of the job. Took his two kids and moved to San Diego. He took it hard. Drank for awhile. When he finally noticed Stacey—Officer Wilbur—he straightened up and started pursuing her."

Mindy brought their drinks and sat them on the table.

Vaughn took a deep draw on his beer. Tasted great. "I needed that. What's your story? You married?"

A shadow crossed Butler's face. "Was once, didn't work out." He sipped his beer and stared over Vaughn's shoulder.

Probably too soon to ask any questions about that. Anyway, he could probably find out from someone else. "Where do you live?'

The two pink spots on Butler's cheeks flamed red. "I'm renting a room from Milligan."

Vaughn couldn't help feeling sorry for the guy. With those cheeks, he couldn't hide his feelings. Interesting. Vaughn took another pull on his bottle. "Really?"

"Yes, but as soon as Doug and Stacey get married, I'll be renting from her parents."

Vaughn's curiosity must have been apparent in his expression because Butler took another swallow of beer and began explaining.

"When my wife kicked me out, I didn't have anywhere to go. Doug took pity on me and rented me a room in his place. When he and Stacey started getting serious, Doug asked me to move, but I couldn't find anything. Her parents have offered to rent me a room as soon as he and Stacey tie the knot." He ran his finger down the side of his bottle. "I suspect Stacey suggested it."

This guy was pitiful. It was obvious that he'd had a thing for Wilbur too. Her parents were probably taking him in to get him out of the engaged couple's hair. "I don't see any of the guys I've met at the department here. Is there another place they hang out?"

Butler shrugged. "This is the only one I know about. I don't drink much."

Vaughn finished his beer and signaled the waitress for another.

"I'm good." Butler glanced at his watch and put his hand over the top of his beer. "In fact, it's time I got going."

No point in arguing, the guy was a wuss, not someone Vaughn wanted for a close friend. "Thanks for showing me this place."

"No problem." Butler stood and acted like he couldn't get out of the bar fast enough.

When Mindy brought Vaughn his second beer, he asked, "Is this joint always so quiet? I was hoping to find the cop hang-out. Is this it?"

"We're usually busier on the weekend, but then it's usually a younger crowd. We used to have more cops coming in. Now it's mostly retired guys like those two at the bar."

After she left, he began to wonder if he'd made a mistake transferring to Rocky Bluff P.D. He'd wanted a place with less action, where he wasn't faced with making life or death decisions all the time. But he wasn't dead yet and needed some diversion in his life. He'd try it out here for awhile; if necessary he could always move on. He finished his beer and headed toward the beach and the cheap motel where he rented a room by the month.

■

Abel had only been at work for about an hour, going through e-mails, faxes and bulletins sent out to notify police departments about wanted felons and unusual crimes in other areas, when one caught his eye.

Young women had disappeared over the last nine months, beginning in the state of Washington and moving down through Oregon. All of the disappearances had happened in coastal communities. So far, no bodies had turned up. The latest reported disappearance was in the town of Whitethorn on the far northern coast of California. The missing woman was twenty-six, worked as a waitress and was the mother of a toddler. Not too many more details.

Might be interesting to learn more about these cases and see what they had in common. He remembered what Maria had told him about his mother and that concerned him more than the cases of the missing women. He went to a search engine on the computer and typed in Alzheimer's.

CHAPTER 2

NOTHING MUCH WAS happening in Rocky Bluff that night. None of the men patrolling the city had spotted anything unusual. No 911 calls received and the operators fought to stay alert. Even though it was getting late, Abel decided to call his brother, Juan, to see if he'd noticed anything different about their mom. He knew his brother seldom went to bed before *The Late Show* was over. Juan answered on the first ring and Abel could hear the TV in the background.

"Hey, Juanito, it's Abel."

Concern sounded in Juan's voice, "Did something happen to mom?"

Odd that he should ask that.

"No, but it's mom I wanted to talk about."

"Oh, yeah?"

"Yeah. I wondered if you'd noticed anything different about her lately."

There was a long pause before Juan said, "As a matter of fact Veronica and I have been concerned about her."

"Have you mentioned this to anyone else? Like dad, for instance?"

"No, but maybe it's time."

At that moment, everything else dropped in importance to Abel. Finding out if Maria was right about his mother became his first priority.

■

Vaughn Aragon's first call of the day was to investigate a reported burglary. There'd been several similar crimes over the last couple of weeks, always one of the expensive homes on the bluff. This was the fourth such call he'd taken. He was beginning to wonder if the people in Rocky Bluff were a bit dense. So far, not a single burglar had needed a tool to break inside a house. There'd been no evidence of forced entry in any of the cases. This was a small department and there was no such thing as a burglary detail; whoever was available took care of the calls—and it seemed he was always available.

The first one he'd investigated, the burglar had obviously strolled right in through an unlocked side door to the garage. Jewelry, flat screen TVs, computers, and money were among the missing items.

Approaching the address of the latest target, he could see that like all the homes in the affluent neighborhood, this one was unique and obviously owned by someone with money—a big white house with narrow windows and a massive chimney. Dark wood embellished the outside walls. It was a Tudor-style home. The only reason Aragon knew that was because while he still tried to placate his ex-wife, she'd dragged him along to look at many houses that were way out of their price range. They'd finally settled on a small pre-World War II stucco bungalow in one of L.A.'s suburbs. Of course, it was awarded to her in the divorce settlement.

Before he could ring the bell, a tall, slim middle-aged woman opened the door. Her perfectly arranged hair had been lightened and she had the tight skin of someone who'd had a recent facelift. Wearing what Aragon suspected was an expensive outfit—a beige waist-length blouse and dark brown slacks, with high-heeled sandals on her feet, she appeared a bit shaken, though in control.

"Officer, am I glad to see you." She put her hand on his arm as if to steady herself. "I think I may have surprised the burglar in the act."

He frowned and peered around her. "What makes you think that?"

She opened the door wider to allow him in. Like the exterior of the house, the furnishings and decor screamed money. Still clinging to the crook of his elbow, she led him into the large living room. The furniture was an eclectic mix of probable antiques and plush modern couches and chairs of different shades of brown with bright splashes of color provided by an array of pillows, but things were in obvious disorder. A flat screen TV sat on the floor, cords still attached. She didn't have to say anything more. It was obvious that she'd interrupted the burglar's activity.

"Come with me." She spun on her heel. He followed her through the formal dining room and into the huge kitchen. "Look there." She pointed toward French doors. Ajar, they opened onto a brick patio. Two pillow cases, bulging with loot, some of it spilling out, sat beside two laptops.

"I didn't touch anything. It's exactly as I found it." She smiled, showing perfect teeth.

"I assume this is how they got in." He moved closer to the door and peered at it. No sign of forced entry.

Underneath her makeup, the woman's face crimsoned. "I went for my regular hair appointment. I didn't feel the need to lock everything. After all, this is considered to be a safe neighborhood."

"Ma'am, haven't you been reading the paper?" He tried to keep irritation out of his voice.

"I don't take the local paper. We only read the national news online."

"Too bad, because if you'd been watching the local TV station or reading the *Banner*, you'd know there've been a rash of burglaries right here in your 'safe' neighborhood." He couldn't resist a little emphasis on the word safe. "The burglar or burglars have been taking advantage of the fact that too many of the residents up here on the bluff tend to leave doors unlocked and garages open. The fact they hit your house in the daytime shows they're getting braver. You're fortunate they left when they heard you come in. You need to realize, now they know what you've got and they'll probably make another attempt. I recommend you be more diligent about locking up. Even better, you ought to consider contacting a security service for an alarm system."

The suggestion of a recurrence rattled the woman's composure, but it didn't last long. She blinked her eyes, swallowed hard, and her demeanor changed. "What's wrong with you police? If there's been several burglaries, why haven't you caught whoever's doing this? Why don't you take fingerprints and find them that way? You know, do some actual police work."

He bristled, but tried to keep himself under control. "Ma'am, we haven't been able to find any fingerprints. Of course, I'll try, but it's obvious that whoever is doing this wears gloves. I think I might have better luck talking to your neighbors to see if anyone has seen any vehicles around they didn't recognize." What sympathy he'd felt for her in the beginning had dissipated.

She tapped her heel on the polished wood floor. "You won't find anyone home. Most of my neighbors work in order to support their life styles. Why don't you people put more patrols in our neighborhood? Wouldn't that discourage the riff raff who are obviously responsible for the break-ins?"

"Rocky Bluff is small and so is our department. We patrol the whole city, but we don't concentrate on merely one neighborhood. You were extremely fortunate not to have been confronted. Take my advice and lock up whenever you go out. If you see any vehicles around you don't recognize or think don't belong in the neighborhood, give us a call."

He could tell the woman wasn't happy with what he said, but he ignored her even though she followed him around as he went about the business of taking fingerprints. It was a futile exercise because he knew from responding to the previous burglary calls he wouldn't find any that matched in their known criminal data base.

As he worked, he once again wondered if he'd made the right choice, leaving LAPD and his ex behind. He certainly hadn't found anything about Rocky Bluff to make him think his life might improve.

■

Because his brother Juan had to be at work at 8:30, he and Abel and their other brother Mario, who usually worked in construction but didn't have a job at the moment, arrived at their parents' home at seven that morning. Because Maria was getting ready for work, Abel brought Lupita with him. He glanced at her wiggling in her car seat. Her huge eyes were shaped like Maria's but were a unique green, he supposed a mixing of his own unusual blue eyes and her mother's brown. Her skin wasn't as light as Abel's nor as dark as Maria's. As usual, he'd combed his daughter's long, deep brown hair into the only "do" he could manage, a ponytail. Lupita loved to visit her grandmother, and he figured his little girl could keep his mother occupied while the men talked.

Because of the two big white Chevy trucks parked in front of the house, he knew his brothers had arrived. His mother opened the door as he came up the walk. "Abel, your brothers are here. Did you know they were coming? Come here, *mija, dame un beso*." Lupita didn't need an invitation, she was already headed into grandmother's waiting arms. His mother had no trouble scooping up the child and kissing her on both cheeks before setting her back down. Tiny, but mighty, was how he and his brothers described their mother, Carmela Navarro. The matriarch of the family, his mother ruled her own household and tried, without success, to rule the households of her sons.

Abel studied his mother with a critical eye. She always wore her hair in a neat up do, fastened with tortoise shell combs. Today, it seemed, more tendrils of graying hair escaped than usual. She wore an apron over a housedress—not unusual, she collected them, different colors and designs. This apron was soiled. He couldn't remember her ever wearing a dirty apron. Always when the one she had on got the tiniest smudge on it, she donned a fresh one—something her daughters-in-law found amusing.

"Did you know your brothers were coming over?" Carmela asked again.

"Yes, Mama, I did. Do you think you could entertain Lupita for me, so we can talk?"

"Of course. How is Maria? Still working at the hospital?" She pursed her mouth and her nostrils flared. She didn't think any mother should work and let her feelings be known in many different ways.

"Yes, Mama. Where are dad and my brothers?"

"Out back by the Koi pond, *por supuesto*. *Aye,* your papa and those fish. Grab yourself a cup of coffee on your way. Did you know your brothers were coming over?"

Again with that question. He shook his head. "Yes. Please keep an eye on Lupita, Mama."

"Of course. Come on, *mija*, I just took some cookies out of the oven."

Lupita took her grandmother's hand. Abel followed behind them into the big kitchen where his mother created her delicious meals. The tantalizing fragrance came from two racks of freshly baked cookies.

"It's kind of early for Lupita to be eating cookies."

"And your Maria wouldn't like that."

"Probably not. You can give Lupita two cookies, but no more, okay?" He held up two fingers.

"Whatever you say, *mijo.*"

His mother lifted Lupita into a chair and turned to the refrigerator and opened it. She turned for a moment and frowned at Abel. "Did you know your brothers were coming over?"

"Sure did, mama. Why don't you pour Lupita some milk to go along with the two cookies you're going to give her?"

"Do you want some *leche* too, *mija*?"

"Please," Lupita said.

Abel poured a cup of coffee and snagged one of the delicious smelling cookies for himself. "Be good for your grandma, sweetie. And Mom, remember only two cookies." He hurried outside, not wanting to hear his mom ask him the same question one more time.

He joined his father and brothers in the redwood gazebo that looked over the Koi pond. Small in stature, today his dad seemed tiny and beaten-down. Abel sat beside him on a bench, hugged him around the shoulder and kissed his sun-darkened and wrinkled cheek. "How's it going, Pop?"

"What do you think?" his dad's voice was low and hoarse. "You boys called for this meeting. What's this all about?"

"We wanted to talk to you about mom," Abel said, peering at his two brothers who both had taken a great interest in their shoes. Juan was the youngest, and often called Juanito since he was named after his father. Though it was more usual for the first born to be named after the father, the story was that his mother had all their names picked out long before she even married their father and she told the nurses what to put on the birth certificates when each of her sons was born. Juan resembled Abel the most. Mario, the eldest, was bigger than either of his brothers, both in height and stature.

"Yeah, about mom," Juan agreed.

Mario nodded.

Abel waited, but neither of his brothers seemed ready to offer anything to the conversation. "Have you noticed anything different about her lately?"

"Like what?" His father sounded defensive. "She's getting older? Me too."

Abel said, "It's more than that, Pop. She just asked me the same question three times, and it isn't the first time I've noticed her doing that."

Juan took a deep breath. "She's losing it. She's gotten lost at least two times that I know about, trying to find someplace she's been hundreds of times."

"How do you know this?" Their father asked without any expression in his voice.

"Because she called Veronica to come and rescue her. Who knows how many other times she might have gotten lost."

"Dad, there must be something really wrong," Mario said.

Still sounding like he didn't believe them, their father said, "She's a little confused sometimes. Old people get like that, you know. I'm confused sometimes. Doesn't mean anything."

"Maria thinks she's showing signs of Alzheimer's." There, he'd said it. Abel sighed loudly.

His father crossed his arms and his ankles. "We all know your wife doesn't like your mother."

"It's more the other way around." Abel struggled to keep his voice calm. "But in any case, Maria says you need to take mom to a doctor. Make an appointment for some tests. If Maria is right there's some new medications that can help if they are started soon enough."

Mario reached over and gripped his father's shoulder. "You should do it, Dad."

At first the older man's dark, wrinkled face remained impassive, but suddenly things changed dramatically. He blinked his eyes a couple of times and tears streamed over his sunken cheeks. He moaned. "Carmela is my life. She is my love. This family can't do without her."

"We don't have to, but she needs help and the sooner she gets it the better." Juan patted his father's hand.

The tears continued to flow. "How do I talk to her about this?"

Abel shrugged. "Not sure. Maybe you shouldn't talk to her at all. Make the appointment and take her."

"Who do I make the appointment with? Carmela is the one who takes care of our doctor appointments."

"Maria can do it for you. She'll know who to call, she'll know who is best." Abel said.

His father wiped his eyes with the back of his hand. He fished in his pocket and brought out a white handkerchief and blew his nose. "I don't want to believe anything is wrong."

Abel stood. "I've got to take Lupita home. I'll let Maria know you want her to make an appointment."

His brothers rose too, murmuring their own reasons to leave.

"Yes, okay." Their father pushed himself to his feet, looking diminutive surrounded by his sons.

"It'll get better, Dad," Mario said.

Their father only nodded.

"You'll see. Once she gets some medicine, mom will be back to her old self." Juan hugged his dad and the others did the same.

On his way back into the house to get Lupita, Abel hoped they weren't being too optimistic. There was something else, something he knew he ought to remember, but all he could think of was getting Lupita and going home. He and his brothers had accomplished what they came for.

When he entered the kitchen, Lupita still sat on the high stool at the kitchen counter where he'd left her. An empty glass with a tiny bit of milk in front of her. One whole rack of cookies was nearly empty. He hoped Lupita wasn't the only one who'd been eating them. The kitchen seemed unusually warm.

His mother glanced at him and asked, "Oh, hello, Abel."

"Are you still baking?"

"No, I'm all through."

He walked over to the stove. "You forgot to turn off the oven." He'd like to reprimand his mom for giving Lupita too many cookies, but he knew it wouldn't do any good.

"Oh, I thought I had. Did you know your brothers were coming over?"

■

After getting Lupita settled in front of the TV watching her favorite DVD, one that she'd watched at least fourteen times already, he called Maria.

Fortunately, she was manning the surgical nurses' station and answered the phone. "Rocky Bluff Memorial, Surgery."

"Hi, honey, it's me."

"Hi, Abel. How did the meeting go with your father?"

"Better than expected. He didn't want to talk about it, of course, but it soon became apparent he's been worried about mother too."

"Good. Is your dad going to make an appointment?"

"He has no idea who to call. Even if he did, I'm not sure he'd ever get around to it. He doesn't really want to face up to what might be happening with mom. Do you think you could do it for him...and me?"

"Of course I'll do it. How did your mom seem to you?"

He tried to keep his emotions in check. "You were right, of course, she's got problems. I don't know why we didn't notice before this."

"Because you don't pay attention to details. I can bet your father has noticed and just didn't know what he ought to do." She sounded more like a nurse than his wife until she added, "No one wants to admit that his wife's mind is going."

Abel knew she was right. "So you'll make the appointment?"

"Yes, then I'll give your dad a call and let him know when and where."

"Thanks, honey, I appreciate it."

"How's Lupita doing?" He assured her all was well, knowing better not to say anything about the cookies.

After he and Maria concluded the conversation, he decided to take Lupita for a walk. In the back of his mind, he had the nagging feeling there was something important he was forgetting—something he should have followed up on.

■

CHAPTER 3

"DID YOU HEAR the news?" was the first question Doug asked when Stacey answered her cell phone.

"What news? I've been busy all day making sure everything is taken care of for our wedding." Stacey had spent most of the day calling the women of the church to thank them for promising to provide food for the reception after the wedding—and also as a reminder.

She'd tried on her dress again, for the thirtieth time, making sure it still fit. She loved her dress and it had taken her a long time to find it. She and her mother had gone all the way to Los Angeles to peruse many up-scale bridal and garment shops. Nothing she'd seen appealed or seemed appropriate for a small, second wedding. Finally, on a whim, she'd popped into a local dress boutique and found the perfect gown, light blue with simple lines made of a light, flowing material that brought the word "gossamer" to mind. It had a scoop neck and reached just below her knees.

Her last stop had been at the florist to make sure the small bouquet, a nosegay, she'd ordered would be ready on time. Stacey couldn't remember the name of the delicate flowers, but they matched the pale blue of her dress.

Doug's only job was to pick up the bridal bouquet and the matching boutonnière on his way to the wedding. She'd remind him early Saturday morning.

Her mom and friends had made darling favors for the tables at the reception using blue ribbons nearly the color of her dress, tied to tiny glass vases filled with clear and light blue pebbles.

She was so excited it was hard to concentrate on much of anything else.

Though she and Doug had decided to marry some time ago, it seemed that one thing or another happened to delay their plans. Over the Christmas holidays, Davey kept getting one sore throat after another, the last one turning into a strep infection. The doctors decided once he was over that, it was time to take out his tonsils.

Stacey didn't really want to be married during winter, though the weather was seldom bad in the beach community, but they'd been having an unusual amount of rain and she'd dreamed of a sunny day for the ceremony. Doug was getting impatient, so they finally decided on a Saturday near the end of March—this coming Saturday.

Once again, Doug interrupted her thoughts. "Are you paying any attention to me at all?"

"I don't guess I'll be much good to anyone until after the wedding. I'm so sorry. Will you tell me again?"

"There was another incident at the beach this morning and the chief wants Strickland to issue a warning to women who jog there. He's supposed to do it on the evening news and it'll be broadcast on the local radio station too."

"Won't that scare away our bad guy?"

"I hope so, but he might not hear it, especially if he doesn't watch our local channel. Not everyone does, you know."

Stacey giggled. "You're right about that. I sometimes think my folks might be the only ones who do."

"Did the chief have anything to say about the plan to have me jog along the beach with Aragon as back-up?"

"He thought it was a good idea, even though I tried to talk him out of it."

She couldn't believe he'd do that. "You did what?"

"Don't get yourself all excited, Stacey, I don't like the idea of you putting yourself out there as a decoy. Who knows what this guy might do."

"He hasn't hurt anyone. He's more of an annoyance than anything else, and he needs to be stopped. Once the business owners and the city council members realize how he could hurt tourism, they'll be ranting for us to do something about him." She paused before adding, "Remember this really is a part of my job so I can take care of crimes like this."

Doug's sigh was loud. "I knew nothing was going to deter you. All I can hope for is the creep will hear the news and move on to another beach community."

"With any luck we'll catch him tomorrow and that'll be the end of it."

"What I really called about is to see if you wanted to go out for awhile this evening."

"Oh, Doug, I just can't tonight. For one thing, I'm beat, and tomorrow I need to get up early and meet Aragon so we can plan how we're going to catch this sick-o." She would've loved to spend some time alone with Doug. Since they'd decided on a date for the wedding, they'd had less and less opportunity to be alone together. Davey's illness, operation and recovery had taken a lot of her time, though Doug had been with her at the hospital and often visited Davey at home. Now that Davey was back in school, she wanted to spend time with her son in the evening, find out what he was learning, and who his friends were. Stacey appreciated her fiancé even more because he was a trooper about taking Davey along with them when they had a free weekend to do something together.

"Okay, I'm not happy, but I understand."

Doug's response reminded Stacey why she loved him so much.

He added hopefully, "Maybe tomorrow night."

She knew her answer would be disappointing. "Maybe, but sweetheart, the closer it gets to our wedding day the less time I'm going to have. Think of it like this, after Saturday we'll be married and we can be together all the time. Let's look forward to the week we'll have off afterwards."

They hadn't made arrangements for a honeymoon, except to take Davey to Disneyland. Part of their time off, they'd have to spend moving Gordon out of Doug's house and moving her and Davey into it. Their plan was to do it in a day with the help of some of their friends from the department.

■

Felix Zachary doubted he'd still be in law enforcement if it hadn't been for his wife. Wendy. As he'd been told by his sergeant and again by the police psychologist, "If you can't imagine yourself in a situation where you'd be willing to resort to lethal force to save your life or that of another, you need to leave the job now."

For awhile, he wasn't sure what he'd do. Not good, because he would be a risk to himself and others around him. He hoped this new guy, Aragon, didn't have a similar problem about using his gun when needed.

After he'd killed the unarmed kid, Felix had horrible nightmares. He'd resisted going to the police psychiatrist, because he was sure he'd get better on his own. Not only did what happen affect him on the job but it had taken a toll on his love life. His beautiful wife wanted a baby, but he used his reluctance to have a mixed-race child as a cover up for his inability to perform in bed.

He should've known he couldn't fool Wendy. She talked to the psychiatrist on her own and learned impotence was common in a case like Felix's. After she told him what she'd learned, she also gave him the day and time for his first appointment. Finally, he accepted that what happened wasn't his fault. Now, Wendy was five months pregnant with their first child.

When Wendy arrived home from her job as a teacher, Felix greeted her with a kiss and caressed her protruding belly—the doctor promised a little girl. He hoped she'd be as beautiful as her mother. It would be interesting to see how Wendy's fair skin, blond hair and blue eyes would mix with his deep mahogany complexion, black hair and brown eyes. "How was your day?"

"Like most days, busy and the kids were full of beans." She moved toward the kitchen. "Isn't it time for you to leave for work?"

"I've got a few minutes. Can I get you something to drink? Hot chocolate? A glass of milk?"

"No, I don't need anything. Sit with me for a minute. You look like you have something on your mind."

Despite having worked all day, Wendy looked great. Being pregnant agreed with her. At times Felix still couldn't believe that this beautiful blonde lady loved him as much as she said she did. She perched on a stool at the bar where they ate quick meals, and didn't take her gaze off him. "Come on. Out with it."

Felix stood opposite her. He glanced at his watch. "It's this new guy we have at work. Aragon. There's something about him that bothers me."

She tilted her head, obviously interested in what he had to say. "What?"

"It's hard to describe. He acts a lot like I did when I was having my problem."

"You mean after you killed that unarmed man."

"Exactly."

"Do you know if that's what happened with him?"

"No. I don't know much about him at all. I just have this feeling." He let his voice trail off as he thought about Aragon.

"Is he married? Maybe I could talk to his wife."

"I heard he was divorced. Haven't really talked to him that much."

"Maybe you ought to find out more."

"Yeah, I plan to do that." He glanced at his watch. "Time to go." He cupped Wendy's head and gave her a lingering kiss. He leaned down to kiss her belly. "Good night, Wee One."

They'd decided not to pick a name among the many they'd listed until they saw what their little girl looked like. At least he had.

Wendy didn't feel the same. That was emphasized when she said, "I think we should start calling her Ruby. Your mother would be thrilled. I'm already thinking of her as Ruby." She slid off the bar stool and put her arms around his neck.

"What if she has light hair and skin as pale as yours? What kind of name is Ruby for a little white girl?"

Wendy's blue eyes crinkled and she giggled. "Chances of that happening are slim. Besides, Ruby is a perfectly good name for a little girl, white, black or half and half. I told you, old-fashioned names are popular right now."

He inhaled Wendy's scent, lemony and some light flowery fragrance that seemed to come from her pores. "I still want to wait."

"You are one stubborn man, Felix Zachary, and I love you." Her blue eyes twinkled. "You watch yourself out there tonight."

As he drove to work he thought about Wendy. She was every bit as stubborn as he, perhaps more so. If she hadn't been, they'd never have married. Both sets of parents were extremely vocal about why their marriage wouldn't work, race being the primary reason.

Felix had been ready to cave, but not Wendy. She blithely planned the wedding, extending invitations to relatives on both sides. After the union, their families didn't immediately become friendly, but they acted civil to one another. Now with news of the impending birth of a first grandchild on either side, they were warming up to one another.

When Wendy kept insisting on naming their baby after his mother, he said, "Don't you think that might alienate your mom?"

Always ready with an answer, Wendy grinned. "That's easy, her middle name will be Elizabeth after my mom."

Felix still wasn't sure if that would be good enough.

Once he arrived at the station and donned his uniform in the locker room, he searched for Lieutenant Stafford.

Near retirement, Stafford was known as a "by-the-book" officer. Stafford had been on the Rocky Bluff P.D. long enough to choose his shifts, but he told everyone the four to midnight was his favorite because there was more action.

Felix stopped Stafford before he went into the squad room where everyone met for the shift change. "Got a minute, Lieutenant?"

"What's on your mind, Zachary?" Stafford squinted at him. His piercing fixation always made Felix feel like the man was trying to peer into his soul.

"What's the story on this new guy, Aragon?"

"Not much, had good references from LAPD. As much as they can legally tell you these days, I suppose. Why?"

Felix shrugged. "Nothing, really, just curious."

Stafford stared at him a few seconds longer as if willing him to say more. Finally he turned and entered the squad room. Felix followed.

■

The aroma from the kitchen was overpowering. Ryan Strickland sometimes wondered if he loved his wife's cooking as much as he loved Barbara herself. When she brought out the golden roast chicken and put it in front of him to slice, he began to salivate. Already on the table was a huge bowl piled high with mashed potatoes, a large tureen of golden gravy, green beans, and a large lettuce salad. Freshly baked biscuits peeked out from under a red-and-white checked tea towel over a basket.

"What's the occasion?" Ryan asked. Usually weeknight dinners consisted of spaghetti, lasagna and other Italian dishes that her first husband had favored and the boys liked. Weekends Barbara was more apt to fix what he thought of as more American-style foods.

"Nothing special," Barbara said. "Shall we bless the food?"

Ryan stared at her. Her lips were lifted in a curious half smile.

The boys crossed themselves quickly and mumbled grace. Philip, the youngest, snagged a biscuit.

"Now that you've helped yourself, Philip, pass the biscuits to your brother." Barbara dished up a spoonful of green beans and handed the bowl to Tony, the eldest of her boys.

"Send your plates down here and I'll cut some of this chicken for you." Ryan concentrated on his chore but couldn't help wondering what was going on with Barbara. "I know you want a drumstick, Philip. You too, Daryl?"

The food was distributed among the family and for a few moments all that could be heard were the sounds of eating and the clinking of silverware against the plates.

"How was your day, Ryan?" Barbara asked.

He tipped his head and stared at her, wondering if she really wanted to know, she wasn't acting her usual self. "Fairly routine. There's been another robbery up on the bluffs. It's a mystery to me why those people can't lock up their houses when they go out. Tonight the local TV station is going to run a public service announcement I made warning female runners not to jog alone."

"H'mm." Barbara took a bite of her biscuit and chewed.

It was unusual for her not to act more interested in what was going on.

After she swallowed, she turned to Tony. "What about you, son? Did you have a good day at school?"

Since his father's death, Tony had been old for his age. Now, at thirteen, he looked like his father. Dark-haired and eyed, he had Al Bertalone's bulky build. "Yeah, Mom." It was obvious he was more interested in eating than talking.

"What about you, Daryl?"

She wasn't giving up.

He put down the drumstick he'd been gnawing on. "We're going on a field trip."

"That's nice. Where to?"

Daryl obligingly answered a few more of his mother's questions before she turned to Tony.

Her interrogation finished, she smiled sweetly at Ryan and placed her hands in her lap.

He blinked. What was she waiting for? Then it dawned on him. "Oh, and how was your day, sweetheart? Anything new going on with your friends?"

"As a matter of fact, yes. I'm surprised you haven't heard."

"Heard what?" He couldn't imagine that there was anything going on in Rocky Bluff that he hadn't heard about, but he soon found out he was wrong.

■

CHAPTER 4

"DID YOU MANAGE to get everything done that you planned?" Clara Osborne, Stacey's mother, asked from the kitchen as Stacey entered the house. "I saved your dinner for you. It's in the oven."

"Mommy, Mommy, you're home." Davey jumped up from the carpet where he'd been watching television and rushed to hug his mother. "Guess what? I learned how to hang upside down from the monkey bars today."

"Wow, that's quite an accomplishment."

"Joey tried to do it and fell on his head."

"Did he get hurt?"

"No. He was mad."

"What else did you learn today?" Stacey hoped to hear something educational from her first grader.

Davey giggled. "That Mrs. Pruitt wears a wig." She was the principal of Davey's school.

"My goodness, how'd you ever find that out?"

"It was on crooked and I saw her other hair peeking out."

"You are truly observant. You might grow up to be a police detective like Doug."

Her father had been watching from his recliner where he'd been reading his newspaper. He lifted his bushy gray eyebrows. "Takes after his mother."

"Hi, Dad." She ran her hand over Clyde's bristly military haircut and kissed him on the forehead.

Clara stood in the doorway of the kitchen. Her salt-and-pepper bob curled around her plump face. "Come on, sweetie, I put your dinner on the table."

While Stacey ate, her mother asked, “So, are you ready for the big day?”

“As ready as I’m going to be.”

“Too bad you have to work the next two days.”

“I think so too. But I’d rather have time off after the wedding than before.”

“Of course you would. I just think it’s too bad you and Doug don’t have more time to be together now.”

“Hey, Stacey, come take a look at this,” Clyde called from his spot in front of the TV. “Your friend Strickland is going to make an announcement.”

The local news was on and she wasn’t surprised to see the backdrop of the Rocky Bluff P.D. About six foot two, the movie-star handsome Strickland was dressed in a gray suit with a black shirt and gray tie. His brief smile revealed perfectly straight teeth.

In a deep, well-modulated voice, Strickland said, “You may have heard, four times in the last two weeks, women jogging along the beach have been accosted by a white male. In most cases, the suspect exposed himself to the victims while making obscene gestures and comments. He also reached out and touched one of his victims. All of these cases have occurred during early morning hours. We suspect there may have been more incidents of this type which haven’t been reported.”

Strickland cleared his throat before adding reassuringly, “The Rocky Bluff P.D. is investigating these crimes and is taking steps to catch the suspect. In the meantime, whenever you’re jogging, we ask that you take the following precautions. Find someone to jog with. Never jog alone. When walking or running along the beach, or anywhere else for that matter, stay aware of your surroundings, know who and what is around you. Don’t be listening to the radio or your iPod. If something doesn’t look or feel right, turn around or go another way. Carry a whistle with you and don’t be shy about using it. Please report any suspicious persons to the Rocky Bluff Police Department.” He closed by listing several telephone numbers.

Reporters began shouting out questions, but Clyde switched off the TV. “Did you know about that, hon?”

Stacey nodded. “Oh yes. I’m supposed to go jogging early tomorrow to try to flush the guy out, but that announcement probably scared him off.”

“Are you still going?”

"Sure, maybe he doesn't watch our local news or he missed the announcement on the radio."

Clara popped out of the kitchen. "Isn't that going to be dangerous?"

"One of the other officers will be watching. Hopefully we can catch this guy and make the beach safe again. Don't forget, this is what my job is all about." Stacey had her doubts about whether or not this would be a futile exercise. She did wish Strickland had waited a day to put out his warning and given them a chance to nab the suspect. If he'd heard the message, all he'd do now would be wait until people forgot about him, then he'd be back at it again.

"Frankly, I hope you catch the guy," Clyde said.

Stacey smiled at her dad. "Me too."

Later that evening, Doug called Stacey. "Since I haven't heard from you, I suppose you're not up to going out."

"I don't think I better. I haven't had much time to spend with Davey. Remember, tomorrow I'm going jogging on the beach. I probably should get a good night's sleep. In the off chance our guy shows up, I want to be at my best."

She could hear the disappointment in Doug's voice. "I'll sure be glad when we're married. Maybe then I'll get to see you once in awhile."

"Sweetheart, it won't be long now. I love you."

"Love you too. Be careful tomorrow."

■

Felix turned the corner onto Valley Boulevard and gasped. "What's going on?"

The dispatcher hadn't put out any information about trouble anywhere and yet the street was congested. It was as bad as a Friday night after a high school football game. Not only that, the sidewalks were crowded with people dashing toward a destination he couldn't figure out.

He turned on his light-bar and touched his siren lightly, hoping the cars in front of him would pull over and let him through. Most obliged as he rolled slowly forward. He squinted to see what was happening up ahead.

It was after seven and the streetlights were on. Some fog had moved in from the ocean, but visibility was good. Except for a couple of bars and restaurants, he knew everything was closed on the two or three blocks ahead. Ideas flooded through his brain—a fight? A dead body? But how would so many people know about it and not the police department? A major accident? No, someone would have called it in. What else could draw such a crowd?

As he moved slowly down the street, he studied the people—all kinds of folks were headed in the same direction: old, young, male, female, Hispanic, white, blacks, and a few kids. What on earth was the attraction?

He called the dispatcher. "Have you heard about anything happening on Valley Boulevard?"

The answer was negative. He explained what he knew, which wasn't much, and asked for back-up.

Finally, he reached the place where the crowd gathered. As far as he could tell, it was nothing but the front window of a furniture store. Fathers lifted their youngsters and pointed. Some held up cell phones to take photos; others made calls. Whatever it was, the word was quickly spreading. Felix glanced in his rearview window and could see a line of headlights behind him. In back he spotted emergency flashers, his back-up.

He drove to the other side of the store and there were just as many people and cars coming from the other direction. He pulled into the only empty spot he could find, beside a fire hydrant. He left his light bar on, climbed out of the police car and joined the people on the sidewalk. "Can someone tell me what's going on here?"

The folks nearest him stared suspiciously and kept moving towards the store front without saying anything. The sidewalk could no longer hold everyone, and some now stood in the street. Not good.

"Folks, you're going to have to move along."

No one paid any attention to him as they pressed closer to one another.

He spotted a familiar face through the crowd. Ryan Strickland. A curly headed woman and three boys stood beside him. Was that his family with him? Growing more curious. Felix waved an arm and shouted, "Strickland. What's happening here?"

Ryan elbowed his way through the throng, which really didn't pay any more attention to him than they had Felix. "It's crazy out here. My wife insisted we come and bring the boys."

"What is it?"

"People think they see an angel in the window. Some think it's Michael or Gabriel."

"Did you see it?"

"Haven't been able to get close enough yet."

"How did she hear about it?"

"She told me all the women at church are calling everyone they know. They think it's some kind of supernatural sign from God."

Felix raised his eyebrows. "Odd."

"I'll have to see it before I believe it. I heard the *Banner* is sending someone down to cover the story."

Felix chuckled. "Of course. This is big news for Rocky Bluff."

"I've got an idea. Since you're in uniform, let's move people out of the way so we can see what all the excitement is about."

Felix and Ryan stood taller than most of those gathered around the store front. "Move out of the way, folks. Coming through. Excuse us." Felix led the way. With reluctance, those in his path moved just enough for the two men to squeeze their way through to the store.

What Felix expected to see was a small reflection in the shape of an angel, something that resembled a Christmas tree topper. Instead, what he saw shocked him.

A full figure nearly covered most of the large surface of the display window. Shiny white with a massive wingspan, the angel, or whatever it was, had masculine features with an unusual, peaceful expression. It, or he, wore a flowing garment. The whole image was so bright it almost hurt Felix's eyes to look at it, yet it was mesmerizing. No wonder people flocked to see the angel.

"What do you think is causing this? Is it a trick of some kind?" Ryan asked. "Something to do with the fog, maybe?"

"I have no clue."

Ryan's wife, Barbara, and her sons had managed to wiggle through the crowd.

The boys "oohed" and "ahhed."

"This is truly a blessing direct from God." Barbara smiled, though her eyes glistened with tears.

An elderly man, a Bible cradled in his arms, said, "Acts 2 tells us that in the end times there will be signs and wonders. God is letting us know He's coming."

Another younger man, obviously a skeptic, muttered, "There's got to be an explanation. It's probably the way the streetlight is shining on the glass." He looked from the image on the window across the road for the nearest streetlights.

As far as Felix could tell, the lights didn't really line up in a manner that could cause the reflection, but that didn't mean he thought he was seeing an angel.

All the people standing around made comments about what they saw. A middle-aged woman with a video camera said, "I was here last night and took a video. It looks just the same on my computer and TV screen. It's definitely one of the major angels."

"How long has this thing been here?" Ryan asked.

The woman frowned. "It's not a 'thing'. I have no idea how long the angel has been here. I came for the first time last night and there were only a handful of people. Obviously the word spread. I know I called all my friends."

A commotion came from the back of the crowd. "Police officer coming through," a voice growled and Vaughn Aragon elbowed the crowd this way and that. Though short, his uniform was taut over his well-muscled body. He exuded a commanding attitude and the throng shrank back. When he reached Felix and Ryan, he said, "We gonna disperse the crowd?"

"What're you doing here? Aren't you working the day shift?"

"Was asked to do a double tonight. Guess one of the guys called in sick. Anyway, don't have anything better to do."

"Take a look." Ryan pointed at the angel. "What do you see?"

Aragon moved closer and peered intently, his nose nearly touching the glass. "I dunno, what am I supposed to see? Some kind of weird reflection. Is that what this is all about?"

"Everyone thinks it's an angel," Felix said. "That's why they're so excited. Most of them believe it's some sort of sign from God."

Aragon stepped back and squinted. "Doesn't look like any angel I ever saw before."

The woman with the video camera pointed her dimpled double chin at him. "And just how many angels have you seen, young man?"

Blinking, Aragon frowned. "None really. I meant pictures of angels. This, if it looks like anything at all, seems to be a man."

"For your information, angels are men." She sniffed and shook her head.

"Really? I didn't know that." Aragon didn't look convinced.

"Me neither," Ryan said.

Barbara took hold of Ryan's arm. She spoke softy, but it became obvious that everyone close enough to hear was listening. "Michael and Gabriel are certainly men. When angels came to earth in Biblical times they often were in the form of men."

The people standing nearby nodded.

"Oh, yeah? What do you know." Aragon sounded as though he didn't care much one way or the other. "Don't you think it's about time we cleared everyone out of here?"

"We ought to call the sergeant before we do anything. Navarro's on duty tonight, right?" Before either of the other men could answer, a reporter with a video camera on his shoulder appeared on the scene and immediately began interviewing people.

"Let's move back out of the way," Ryan said. "Make your call, fill Navarro in on the situation, but I think the wisest move would be to stand back. As long as no one is causing any trouble, let them enjoy themselves. This really isn't hurting anyone and if you try to make people leave, all you're going to do is make them angry."

Barbara smiled at the two policemen. "My husband is right. This is a sign from God. There's a reason the angel is here."

Felix nodded. "Come on, Aragon, let's call in and unless we're told different, we can stand by our cars to watch the crowd."

With a smirk on his face, Aragon nodded. "Might as well, nothing else seems to be going on around this burg."

■

Barbara wanted to stay far longer than Ryan. The first time he told her they ought to leave, her answer was, "This is something the boys need to see. Something like this happens only once in a lifetime. It's God exhibiting his presence."

When the boys showed signs of boredom, Ryan tried again. "Tomorrow is a school day. Don't you think it's time we took them home?"

This time she agreed, but kept turning back for one last look at the angel in the window. Ryan might have thought the whole fascination with the appearance was a Catholic thing, since Barbara was Catholic and had heard about it from her church friends, but others spoke about their beliefs and it seemed people from many religions had gathered to see the unusual phenomenon.

No doubt whatever was causing the appearance of the angel would disappear in a day or two and traffic on Valley Boulevard would return to normal.

■

Sergeant Navarro agreed that Officers Zachary and Aragon should make sure all remained peaceful and remain on the scene until the crowd began to disperse. This gave Felix time to get acquainted with Vaughn Aragon. Felix's car was the nearest so they both stood beside it. Aragon crossed his arms and leaned against the door.

"How do you like it here in Rocky Bluff so far?" Felix asked.

"I dunno. Kind of boring."

"If you need action, you should have stayed in L.A. What brought you here anyway?"

A brief shadow crossed Vaughn's face. He lowered his eyelids for a long moment. "Wanted to get away from all the gang violence. Didn't have anything to keep me there since my wife divorced me and was awarded my house in the settlement. Didn't make sense to stay and be miserable."

Felix felt there was more, but Vaughn didn't seem inclined to open up.

"Most of the time it's pretty quiet here in Rocky Bluff though we've had a few murders over the years. Unfortunately, more and more people are moving here from the big cities. More people means more crime."

Vaughn pulled a toothpick out of his pocket and put it in the corner of his mouth. "Wish I'd done a bit more investigating, though before I picked this place."

"What do you mean?" Felix turned his gaze away from Vaughn and surveyed the crowd. It didn't seem to be getting any bigger, but it sure wasn't any smaller.

"So far the only other single guy I've met is Butler. He's a barrel of laughs."

"You're kidding, right?"

"Of course. We went out for a couple of beers and he could hardly wait to get out of the bar. What do cops do for fun around here, anyway?"

"Like you've learned, almost everyone is married. We do stuff with our families whenever we can. Once in awhile someone has a party. We used to have a few old guys that hung out in bars and did a lot of drinking, but times have changed. Being a police officer is more of a profession now."

"Some of that's happened in L.A. too, but there are still some guys looking for a good time now and then. If someone was having a party, the question was, 'Wives or girlfriends?'" Aragon laughed.

"It's not like that here. Most everyone goes home after their shift. Won't be long before I'll be a father. Can hardly wait."

"Oh yeah? That's great, man."

Felix suspected Aragon was being sarcastic. The conversation moved on to more mundane subjects like:

"What is the chief really like?" "How often could they expect a raise?" "Anyone I ought to be watching out for?"

And continued on to, "What's Stacey Wilbur like to work with?"

"She's a great gal and good officer. Much tougher than she looks."

"She's pretty small. What about if she's your back-up when things blow?"

"You'd be surprised at how forceful she can be, physically and mentally. She's taken all the same kind of classes as the rest of the department and is really good in martial arts. Most of the time she doesn't have to resort to that sort of thing, though. She's a genius at talking people down. You're going to be working with her tomorrow, aren't you? Trying to catch that guy who's exposing himself to female joggers?"

"That's the plan if the suspect wasn't scared off by Strickland's broadcast warning people not to jog without a partner."

"He might not show up the first time you're out there, but he'll be back."

Finally the crowd began to thin, and Felix and Aragon were able to leave.

■

Probably wasn't a good idea to drink anything since he had to be up early in the morning to back-up Officer Wilbur, but Vaughn Aragon decided one beer wouldn't hurt and might help him sleep. Sleep didn't come easy these days and when it did, nightmares came with it. He switched on the TV in the seedy room which was now his home, propped a pillow against the cheap wooden headboard and leaned against it. It didn't matter what he watched, anything to divert his mind from thoughts of that dead kid.

Vaughn finished off the beer and set the alarm. Disappointment set in. He hoped for some excitement tomorrow. With some luck, he imagined nailing the guy and gaining some respect from the other guys in the department. No chance of that now since Strickland's broadcasted warning.

These days, things never seemed to work out the way he hoped. No matter how macho he thought himself, shooting that kid robbing the convenience store had affected him more deeply than he'd ever admitted to anyone but himself. Though it had begun like many other calls, a silent alarm at one of the hundreds of small, independent groceries that were tucked into all the diverse neighborhoods that made up the poorer parts of the Los Angeles basin, it didn't turn out the way most of them did. This was the first time he'd reached a store while the robbery was in progress.

Vaughn had responded to his radio dispatch a few minutes after midnight. Only one block from the address, he'd careened into the nearly empty parking lot, jumped out of his police car, pulled his gun, and peeked into the open door of the store. He spotted the robber at the same moment the robber turned and saw him.

From then on it was like a movie—a scene that played and replayed in his mind. The robber was dressed all in black with a ski mask pulled down over his face. Only dark eyes stared out at Vaughn.

At the time, Vaughn had no idea the suspect was only a kid. Vaughn's lone thought was the guy was a threat to him and anyone who might be in the store.

With both hands, he held a big gun pointed directly at Vaughn.

Vaughn ducked out of sight. The kid fired the gun, and fired again.

Screams came from inside the store.

Instinctively, Vaughn darted into the store shooting.

The kid fell.

What Vaughn remembered most were the smells. The acrid odor of gunfire. The coppery scent of the blood that was turning the gray asphalt tile floor a dark crimson. The pungent stench of emptied bowels and bladder. His own perspiration.

Behind the counter, an ancient Asian woman wept.

Vaughn kicked the gun away from the limp hand, though he knew there was no chance it would be fired by the dead assailant. He knelt beside the body and yanked off the ski mask.

His heart dropped and his stomach wrenched. The taste of bile rising in his throat choked him. The dead robber wasn't a man. He was a black youth, probably no more than fourteen or fifteen years old.

As it turned out, the young man was believed to be responsible for a rash of robberies of stores owned and operated by people of different nationalities in a twenty-mile radius. The dead boy's most recent residence was located in the center. He already had a long record as a juvenile offender. None of that information made Vaughn feel any better. He'd killed a kid.

No one blamed him, not even the kid's family. The youth had a history of trouble, starting in grammar school, everything from truancy, assault and battery of a teacher and his own mother, to many breaking and entering charges, physical assaults in group homes and juvenile facilities, and the list went on and on.

None of that mattered, because when Vaughn went to sleep at night, he had nightmares about the youth he'd gunned down. The shooting replayed over and over. He kept seeing that young face. The ruined body. Blood spilled all over the dirty floor.

More than anything else, that shooting had ruined his marriage. Of course, his wife would present other reasons: his indifference, his drinking, not coming home after his shift, suspected infidelity. The last one wasn't true. He could no longer perform as a lover, not with his wife nor with anyone else. That was his biggest problem, one he hadn't been able to bring himself to discuss with the police psychiatrist. She was a woman. A foxy woman at that. How could he talk about something like that with a female?

He'd managed to con the doc into thinking everything was fine, answered all her questions the way he knew she wanted them answered and she'd allowed him back on duty. But, he couldn't hack it. He avoided any call that might result in violence. No way was he going to take another chance of killing a kid. He'd asked for a transfer to traffic control, but the transfer wasn't granted. After a few miserable months, he requested a transfer to the Rocky Bluff P.D. By that time his marriage was over and his bosses were glad to get rid of him.

Now he was here and wasn't feeling any better about himself than he had in L.A. He drained his beer, made sure the alarm was set and turned off the light.

CHAPTER 5

EARLY MORNING FOG made it nearly impossible to see much farther than several feet. Stacey parked her yellow VW bug on the old parking lot. Thick clumps of dry weeds fought their way through the cracked asphalt. The condemned pier eerily disappeared into the gray mist of the ocean and sky. A dangerous nuisance, the rotting wooden structure was also an eyesore. Despite the rusting chain with the crooked "No Trespassing" sign dangling across the entrance, teenagers continued to use it as a place to hang out as evidenced by the discarded beer bottles and other trash scattered on the beach and the parking lot. City fathers talked about tearing down the pier, but anything that cost money and wasn't going to bring in some wasn't a priority.

Aragon wasn't there yet which didn't surprise Stacey. Deciding not to take her gun, she'd locked it and the holster in the glove compartment. She climbed out of the car and immediately wrapped her arms around herself and shivered. In one of the pockets of her light hooded sweatshirt she'd tucked her badge and wrist cuffs, in the other, her cell phone and keys. As always, when working under-cover, she'd left her engagement ring at home.

While doing a few stretches to warm up, she heard the approaching vehicle before she spotted a blue-and-white Rocky Bluff P.D. car appearing almost magically through the gloom.

The unit pulled up beside her bug and Vaughn Aragon stepped out. Dark circles underlined his sunken eyes. "Looks like you're ready. Sorry I'm late. I pulled a second shift yesterday evening."

That was unusual. "What was happening?"

"You didn't hear the news this morning?"

"No, too busy with my son and getting ready."

He filled her in about the angel in the window.

What an incredible story. "Did you see it?"

"Sure."

"What do you think? Is it for real?"

"Nah, it's just some kind of reflection. Strickland's wife was impressed with it, though."

"Barbara's pretty religious." She didn't think it the time or place to discuss her own spiritual beliefs, they had more important things to take care of.

"Figured that. What's the plan for this morning?"

"I'm going to drive back to Seagull. That's the first street to the north with beach access and a good place to leave my car. There are seven streets leading to the beach, all with sea bird names. Albatross is at the far end, the one with the big, expensive seafood restaurant. All of the reported encounters with our suspect were somewhere in between. Go to Sandpiper and park on the street in front of one of the houses. Big sand dunes have piled up all along near the end of the streets where there's parking for people going to the beach. I figure if you go on top of the dune there, you ought to be able to watch me from the time I start jogging until I get to the end and turn around and come back. If our man makes an appearance, I'll talk to him before I identify myself as a police officer. That'll give you time to catch up with us."

"Sounds like a plan to me. I'll find a spot where I have the best view up and down the beach. We're probably wasting our time, but don't worry, I'll be watchful just the same."

Stacey grinned. "Okay. Give me your cell number so I can call you if necessary."

He did and she programmed it into her phone. "At least I'll get some much needed exercise without going to the gym." He didn't need to know that she seldom went to the gym. Chasing after a six-year-old boy kept her moving and she ran three or four times a week, but her preference when she did jog was around the neighborhood where she lived. She was actually looking forward to her jog down the beach because she enjoyed a good run. Like Aragon though, she figured exercise was all she was going to get because of the warning issued over the TV and radio.

Stacey drove out of the lot, headed out to Valley Boulevard and continued all the way down to Seagull. She glanced at the furniture store where Aragon said the angel had been. The sidewalk in front of the store was deserted now, the window blank.

The streets that ran down the hillside toward Valley were named after trees and flowers, but they didn't match up with the streets leading to the beach. It was as though the beach side wasn't a part of Rocky Bluff. Certainly the houses didn't look like the residences that went from Valley up the hill. Built during the early thirties, most of the homes were small and in various stages of dilapidation. Years ago, the owners had used the cottages for their summer vacations. As the owners died off, the homes were sold and now most were used as rentals. Stacey had heard that a developer had discovered Rocky Bluff and planned to buy up most of the beach real estate. The word was that the old houses would be torn down and new, expensive homes and condos built in their place. Though some of the buildings were eyesores, the rent was cheap. Stacey wondered what would happen to the families who lived there if they were forced to move.

Seagull was the last street before the rocky bluff which gave the city its name. Stacey drove past the tiny beach cottages, some with neat, green lawns and flowering bushes, while other yards were neglected, full of weeds and brown grass.

Still too early in the year to attract many beach goers, Stacey found the sandy parking area at the end of the street empty. After locking the VW, and sticking her keys in the pocket of her shorts, she climbed up and over the sand dune. When she reached the top, she could see the ocean, a dismal grayish blue thanks to the low fog. The beach seemed deserted except for the long-legged birds playing tag with the foam that rushed toward them. The sound of the ocean seemed muted just as the fog had dulled the color.

She made her way down to the damp sand, a better running surface. Once more glancing in both directions and seeing no one, she did a few more stretches. Heading south at a quick pace, an euphoria settled over her. She made herself focus. It was essential to stay alert and cognizant of her surroundings.

Her running shoes made a plopping sound on the wet sand. Waves crashed off shore. The foam hissed. Despite the overcast, she could see all the way to the pier. The beach was deserted. Women had paid attention to the warning. Good.

As she ran, she began to perspire, but the fine spray from the waves cooled her. She inhaled the salty air. She fought the urge to give in to the exhilaration that tugged at her. Instead she glanced periodically at the sand dunes, wondering if she could spot Aragon. Her thoughts drifted to her fairly new position as head of the vice squad. What a laugh. The squad consisted of herself and a helper like Aragon, but only when the situation warranted it.

Seagulls swooped down into the water searching for something to eat. The popping of seaweed pods as she stepped on them brought her mind back to where it needed to be.

She had learned a few things in the time she'd had her new job though. It was difficult to find a prostitute on the first and fifteenth when the welfare checks arrived. Unfortunately there was a high incidence of HIV among the women who sold themselves. Unlike the big cities, if they had a pimp it was usually a husband or boyfriend. Children were often farmed out to their grandparents. She hadn't been aggressive about arresting prostitutes.

Her keys jingled in her pocket.

Though she kept an eye out for Aragon, she didn't see him or anyone else all the way to the restaurant that came before the pier. Good place to turn around. On her way back, she thought she spotted the top of Aragon's head once, but it was brief and she wasn't sure it was him. For a moment, she wondered if it might be their suspect, but no one came over the dune.

She'd nearly reached the place where she'd parked her car. A movement startled her. A big Golden Retriever bounded toward her, tail wagging.

Stacey knelt down and rubbed his ears.

A plump woman in a pink sweat suit, a leash dangling from her hand, puffed her way toward Stacey. "I'm sorry. I meant to put the leash on Toby, but he got away from me."

After giving the dog one last pat on the head, Stacey stood. "It's okay, he's a sweetheart. You did hear the warning about the man who's been exposing himself to joggers, right?"

"Oh yes, but I don't think I need to worry with Toby by my side. He seems really sweet, and he is to women, but he's not nearly as friendly with men, especially if Toby thinks I'm in danger."

"It's up to you, of course." Stacey was dubious about the Golden's ability to actually provide any protection, he seemed too friendly. "If you do happen to see anyone who looks the least bit suspicious, turn around and go home."

The woman frowned. "You sound so, I don't know, official."

Stacey smiled. "I'm a police officer." She pulled her badge out of her pocket.

Realization crept into the woman's expression. "Oh, you were out here trying to catch that guy, right?"

"Yes, but I didn't. So be careful."

Stacey glanced at her watch; it was long after the time the suspect usually made his move. She headed toward her car, pulling out her cell phone. She called Aragon. "Hey, I don't think our guy is going to show, but just in case, there's a woman out here with her dog, big Golden Retriever. How about hanging around a bit longer and keeping an eye on her."

"Will do."

Stacey headed back to the station, showered, and changed into a pair of dark jeans and a sleeveless T-shirt she had in her locker. She wrote a quick report on her unsuccessful attempt at catching the suspect, and wondered what she ought to do next.

Doug might be in his office, so she headed in that direction in time to see him and his partner, Frank Marshall, rushing out into the hall. Doug spotted her. "Hey, Stacey, how'd it go this morning?"

"Had a good run, nothing more. What's up?"

"Navarro called in. Seems his mother has gone missing. Did you know she's suffering from Alzheimer's?"

"No, I hadn't heard. What're you going to do?"

"We've got the guys on patrol looking, but Frank and I thought we'd head out and see if we might spot her. Want to come along?"

"Sure. Don't think I've ever seen his mother." Stacey fell in step with the two men as they hurried toward the back door of the station. "What does she look like?"

"She's short like Abel's whole family. Plump, graying hair. Usually wears it on top of her head."

Outside, Stacey said, "I think I ought to go in my own car. No sense in all of us looking in the same places."

Doug's disappointment showed in his expression.

Frank said, "She's right."

"How long has the senior Mrs. Navarro been gone?" Stacey asked.

"That's what no one seems to know. When Abel's dad woke up this morning, she wasn't in their bed. He looked all around the house and she wasn't there. Of course Abel and his brothers are out scouring the neighborhood around their parents' home." Doug opened Stacey's car door for her.

"I just came from the beach and she wasn't there." Stacey slid behind the wheel. "Aragon's still keeping an eye out at the beach. I'll give him a call and tell him to watch for her in that area."

"I thought we'd find out where Abel and his brothers are searching and spread out from there." Doug leaned on the open door. Frank stood behind him.

"Maybe I ought to head up the hill. Go up and down a few streets. Have any idea how she was dressed?"

"Abel's dad thinks she's still in her nightgown. She always wears flannel nightgowns to bed. He didn't seem to know the color, but it shouldn't be too hard to spot an old lady wandering the streets in her nightie." Frank sounded glib, but Stacey knew he was merely trying to make light of a frightening situation.

■

Stacey let the dispatcher know she was joining the search for the eldest Mrs. Navarro and was going in her own car but could be reached on her cell. She also called Aragon to let him know what was going on and to be on the look out. Aragon said, "I'm leaving the beach. The woman with the dog has already headed home. I'll go drive through the bird streets, see if she's down here."

■

Abel remained at the house in an effort to console his father, while his brothers canvassed the neighborhood, knocking on doors and asking if anyone had seen their missing mother. They sat at the kitchen table, while Lupita watched cartoons in the living room.

"*Dios mio*," Abel's father cried out, over and over. "I should have done something sooner. It's my fault. I knew something was wrong and I ignored it."

"No, it's not your fault. No one knew she'd wander off, Pop. Don't worry, we'll find her."

Tears slid down his dad's wrinkled cheeks. His hands trembled.

Abel's phone rang.

It was Maria. "Any news?"

"We haven't found her yet, but everyone's looking, including most of the department."

"Don't worry, Abel, it won't be long until someone spots her."

Abel turned and shielded his mouth as he spoke. "I feel like I ought to be out looking, but I've got Lupita here watching TV and my dad is too upset for me to leave him by himself."

"You're doing the right thing by staying with him. I made an appointment for her. The doctor has the best reputation for working with Alzheimer's patients. Write down the information to give to your father." She gave him the details and Abel wrote them down.

After he hung up, he showed the note to his father before tucking it under the phone on the desk where his mother made out her grocery lists. "Pop, you take mom to see this doctor. He'll know what to do about her problem." Abel prayed it was so.

"What if we don't find her?" Abel's dad seemed to be shrinking.

"We will. Stop worrying. It's only a matter of time." But Abel couldn't help thinking about all the hazards that could befall a confused old woman who didn't know where she was. He grabbed his father's hand and squeezed.

"There's something I need to confess," his father said.

Abel frowned. "You want to go to confession?"

"No, no." His father shook his head. "I need to confess to you."

What on earth was this about? Abel didn't know if he could take much more. First his mother, now his father. "What is it, Pop?"

"Lots of things have been happening to your mom. She hasn't been acting right for a long time." The older man stared at his feet.

"Why didn't you tell us?"

"I didn't want you to think less of your mother."

"We wouldn't. We love her, you know that."

"But she's always been able to do everything." Abel's father's voice quavered.

"What kind of things have you noticed?"

"Your mama doesn't remember how to make tortillas," he wailed.

Abel's mother loved to make tortillas. She was proud of the fact that she always made her own.

His father continued. "She sent me out to buy tortillas. Told me she didn't have time to make them. All the ingredients sat out on the counter, but she just stared at them. When she started throwing everything away, I knew there was a problem."

Understanding, Abel nodded.

"That's not all. She has trouble figuring out what to wear. For the last few months, I've been setting out her clothes. I have to put them in order, the first things on at the top."

His mother was far worse than any of them had known, but he didn't blame his father for trying to hide his wife's condition. Abel knew the old man was just trying to cope with something he didn't understand.

Deep in thought, he jumped when the phone rang.

CHAPTER 6

WHEN BARBARA HEARD the news about Mrs. Navarro, the first thing she did was go to church, light a candle and pray for the woman's safety and quick recovery. While driving there and back, she kept watch for an older woman in her nightgown. At home, she got on the phone and began calling the wives of the Rocky Bluff P.D. asking them to be on the lookout for Abel's mother.

It turned into a morning-long project. Most of the time she merely left a message because so many of the wives worked. When someone did answer, the conversation lasted for awhile as everyone wanted to catch up with the latest P.D. gossip and news.

Detective Marshall's wife, Gwen, was in a talkative mood. After listening to the details about the missing Mrs. Navarro, she asked, "What do you think about the angel people think they're seeing on that window downtown?"

Barbara and Gwen were long-time friends and of course she knew Barbara was Catholic and no doubt suspected she'd visited the site.

"I took the boys and went down to see for myself," Barbara told her.

"Well, is it really an angel?"

"It definitely looks like one, though not what most folks imagine when they think of celestial beings."

"The paper said people think it might be Michael or Gabriel." Gwen didn't sound like she disbelieved or was making fun of the phenomena, merely curious. A cop's wife for years, Gwen had probably seen it all; she was an example for all the wives. Though she didn't work outside the home, she kept busy doing volunteer work with the police wives association and taking classes from belly dancing to body language, and once in awhile a college class, like metaphysics. Like most of the wives, they shared department gossip among themselves but never talked about what was going on with outsiders.

Barbara decided to be honest. "Frankly, I think this is a sign from God, a reminder that He's around and still in control despite all the bad stuff that happens."

"What does Ryan think?"

"He's a cop, so he's skeptical, of course. He's sure it's some kind of reflection that will disappear in a few days. Doesn't matter how or what's causing the vision, or how long it stays, it's clearly a message from God."

"Interesting." Gwen sounded contemplative. "I better let you go. I'll take a walk around my neighborhood and see if Mrs. Navarro might be wandering around here."

After they said their goodbyes, Barbara moved her laundry from the washer into the dryer. She'd either left a message or talked to everyone on her list. Barbara loved being a mother and the wife of a cop. She knew that it took a certain kind of personality to survive this demanding role. Not every woman could handle the fact that when she kissed her husband goodbye, he might not come back. She'd had that happen to her, though in her case, she'd actually been a witness when her first husband, Al, was killed in the line of duty.

She'd been surprised by the strength she'd found within herself after Al's death. Ryan had been assigned to help her out during those dark days. She knew she wasn't the only one who'd been surprised by the special attention he'd given her, long after his assignment ended. Though always competent and organized, Barbara knew most people thought of her as merely a pleasant woman and good mother who talked too much. They were even more surprised, astonished even, when Ryan who was known as a womanizer asked Barbara to marry him. Actually no one was more surprised than she. His good looks had nothing to do with her acceptance. Her boys needed a father and they liked Ryan and he genuinely liked them. During the time he'd helped her with all the details of the funeral, getting the family affairs in order, and trying to keep some semblance of normality for the boys, he'd become a friend. As time passed, their friendship developed into affection, and finally love.

Doug Milligan's marriage had been another casualty linked to Al's death.

Doug's wife, Kerrie, couldn't take the constant fear she had that something might happen to Doug. Al's death was the excuse she used for the divorce. Some women should never marry a man in law enforcement. A wife of a cop needed to be self-sufficient, able to fix or call the repairman for leaky faucets and broken appliances. Refereeing family squabbles and taking care of any problems at home fell under "wifely duties". Christmas, New Year's, and other holidays and family celebrations were often spent without him. Being without your spouse during special moments were the loneliest times of all.

However, balancing household tasks, doctor visits, and chauffeur duties for the boys was second nature to Barbara. When Ryan was home, he helped, but she never counted on him. She was content keeping his home comfortable, cooking his meals, and loving him. When he could, he helped out with everything, but best of all, she knew he loved her back.

■

The meeting with the mayor and city council had given Chief Michael McKenzie a headache. Nothing new, meeting with them always gave him a headache. The Chief sat behind his desk, took off his wire-framed glasses, and massaged his temples. So many things were needed by the Rocky Bluff Police Department, from new police cars to upgraded computers, but the city fathers ignored the department's needs.

Little in the station house had changed over the years. Most of the rooms were utilitarian except for personal decorations added by the men, like family photos, police memorabilia and cartoons. The only reason McKenzie had a nice oak desk was because he'd purchased it himself, along with his comfortable swivel chair. The pale beige drapes, utilitarian chairs upholstered in a muted pattern of several shades of brown and the faded chocolate carpet on the floor had been there since the department first opened its doors. Everything showed its age.

The paneled walls displayed various certificates, diplomas, and awards earned by McKenzie, as well as several original oils of rustic country scenes he'd brought from home.

A sharp knock preceded the entry of Lieutenant Stafford wearing civilian clothes. "Your secretary told me to come in. How'd it go this morning?"

Since the lieutenant had been on Rocky Bluff P.D. as long as the chief, they'd become good friends, often discussing management and personnel problems. The lack of funds provided by the city to upgrade or increase salaries was an on-going topic. As a result, there was a hiring freeze. The only new man in the last year was the transfer from LAPD, and the only reason the council agreed to the transfer request was because there would be no training expense.

"As we expected." McKenzie motioned for Stafford to sit in one of the chairs in front of his desk. "They aren't about to give us any more money. As usual, the worst was Councilman Blandly."

Stafford's steel gray hair was cut short. His tailored shirt and khaki pants sported sharp creases, his dark brown shoes freshly polished. He sat. "Smug jackass. He acts like the money is coming out of his own pocket. Don't those idiot councilmen realize that fewer cops on the street cuts down our ability to have the manpower to solve a major crime? Not to mention keeping everyone safe."

"I once heard someone say, 'It's like juggling. If you try to juggle too many balls at the same time, you're bound to lose a few.' All those bozos could talk about was the man bothering women joggers on the beach, what was taking us so long to make an arrest. Their only concern is how this might affect tourism."

"It's not as if we have an invasion of tourists every year. We're lucky to get a handful. Santa Barbara and Ventura are too close for people to bother stopping here."

"That's what the council is all about these days, luring tourists to visit Rocky Bluff. Their main topic of discussion was tearing down the old houses by the beach and replacing them with condos and upscale homes."

"What happens to the poor folks who live in the rentals down there?"

"None of those high and mighty council members give a damn about that."

Stafford shook his head. "Did you hear the news about Sergeant Navarro's mother?"

Despite being the chief, sometimes he was the last to find out what was going on with his own people. "No, what's wrong?"

"Seems she's suffering from dementia and disappeared from her home sometime last night. We have men looking for her, but she hasn't turned up yet."

"That doesn't sound good. How's Navarro handling this? I know his family's close."

"He's with his father now. As you'd expect, the old man's pretty shook up. Navarro's brothers are out searching for her too."

"Let me know if you hear anything else."

"If they haven't found her by the time I leave today, I'll join the search."

■

Stacey had decided to drive her VW bug for a couple of reasons, one because Mrs. Navarro might be frightened by a police car, and two—the primary reason—there wasn't an official car left in the police yard. Everyone was out looking for Abel's mother.

She called her folks to let them know what was going on. Her father promised to canvas their neighborhood too. Where on earth would an old lady go in the middle of the night? Stacey couldn't think of a rational reason why Mrs. Navarro would leave the safety and comfort of her bed and walk out of her house. No one had ever spoken about the senior Navarros having marital problems of any kind, nor had anyone accused Mr. Navarro of abuse. In fact, what Stacey had heard from Abel's wife, Maria, was that Mrs. Navarro was a bit of a tyrant. She ruled her own household and tried to rule those of her sons.

Troubled by dementia or not, the woman was probably getting hungry by now, having missed breakfast. If she'd wandered around so far she couldn't find her way back home, perhaps she would look for a friendly face or someplace where she might be offered a meal.

Stacey knew the Navarros lived about halfway up the hillside that led to the freeway. Because it was harder to walk uphill than down, she suspected the older woman had taken the easiest path. Stacey could only guess which direction she'd gone, but she knew that Abel's brothers had already started their house-to-house search from their parents' home. No doubt the other officers were working farther afield and had been for at least an hour. Stacey decided to look in the neighborhoods that bordered the bluff.

The nearly perpendicular rock and sandy face of the cliff rose up on the far side of a ravine that only filled with water during the rainy season. Named after the formation, the town spread from the beach up the more gently rising hillside. It wasn't until the last fifteen years that developers began building on the bluff itself. The area quickly became the most exclusive and expensive location for homes. Despite having no beach access, the ocean view was spectacular. Enough so, the city fathers had put in a public walking path before all the land had been turned into private residences.

Stacey felt sure Mrs. Navarro had not been able to make her way up there. She began her search three streets down from the Navarros'. By this time, the brothers had probably been to the houses on both sides of the first two streets. If she started at the far end, and learned neither of the men had been by yet, she'd continue on.

The houses on the street she chose were like so many in this part of town, built in the twenties and thirties, some stucco, others wood. One and two stories, each with its own individual style, but the ones on the high side all had stairs leading to porches. Stacey figured Mrs. Navarro would have avoided the houses with stairs. The ones on the low side of the street had their first story at street level, and a driveway that went down hill to the second floor below and to the garage.

No one was home at the first two houses Stacey visited. At the third, an old man in a tattered bathrobe yanked open the door and glared at her. Before she could say anything, he growled, "Are you blind? Can't you see the sign in front of your nose, no solicitors."

"Sir, I'm looking..."

He slammed the door in her face.

When Stacey rang the bell at the next house, a dog barked furiously from behind a redwood fence close to the entrance. The dog had worked his muzzle through a hole in the slats. He barked, stopping momentarily to chew on the wood around the hole. Sawdust flew as he gnawed off chunks. Surely if someone was home, they'd have come to the door by now.

She hurried across the lawn to the next house.

A young woman with a baby on her jean-clad hip, opened the door with a scowl. A toddler in a droopy diaper and runny nose peeked around her leg.

Stacey displayed her badge and ID. "I'm looking for a missing woman. I wondered if you might have seen her. She wandered away from home sometime last night."

The baby started to howl. The toddler's nose dripped.

"Sorry, I can't help you. My kids are sick and I haven't been out of the house in two days." The door shut.

Stacey tried two more houses where neither knocking or ringing the bell raised any occupants. She moved on to a house with a floor to ceiling window next to the door. Before she even reached the porch, a brown pit bull with a red nose banged against the window, hitting it with all his muscular weight.

Stacey jumped. The dog barked and growled like mad.

She stepped back a few feet, but that didn't calm the dog. He continued to bounce against the window, growling and baring his teeth. Obviously, no one was home but the dog.

The next to the last house on the block, a bit more modern than the rest with lots of glass brick on the front had a redwood door. She pushed the bell and listened to chimes echoing inside. When she was about to give up and move on, she heard footsteps followed by the sound of a lock being turned. The door opened.

A young black woman, perhaps in her thirties, wearing what looked like a nurses' uniform, green smock top and pants and white sneakers, pulled the door open. She frowned. "Yes?"

Again, Stacey showed her ID. "Officer Wilbur, I'm here..."

The woman cut her off. "I bet I know exactly why you're here. You're looking for an older Hispanic lady."

"Yes, ma'am. Have you seen her?"

"I've not only seen her, she's sound asleep in my guest room. I wouldn't have noticed her, except I'm expecting company this weekend. When I got off work, I went shopping and bought some sodas and snacks to put downstairs. I'm afraid I'm not good about keeping the back of the house locked. When I came home just a few minutes ago, I went in there to put the groceries away. What a surprise to see this strange woman curled up on the bed, wearing her nightgown."

"Is she still there?" Stacey asked.

"Yes, I didn't wake her. I came upstairs to call the police when you rang the doorbell. Come on, I'll show you where she is."

Stacey stepped inside the small living room that opened onto a dining area and kitchen. The woman led the way to a staircase off to the side. The lower half of the house held the laundry room, a second smaller kitchen with two grocery sacks sitting on the counter.

The woman pointed out a banana peel and a crumpled chips' bag. "I didn't leave that there. I suspect your missing woman helped herself." They passed a small room that held exercise equipment, a bathroom, and finally, the bedroom.

There, under a handmade quilt, Mrs. Navarro lay peacefully sleeping. Though Stacey couldn't remember seeing her before, this had to be Abel's missing mother.

Stacey took her cell phone from her purse and called the dispatcher. "Officer Wilbur here. I've located the missing woman, Mrs. Navarro." She turned to the homeowner, "What's your address?"

The woman told her.

Stacey repeated it to the dispatcher, adding, "Call Sergeant Navarro first. He's with his father at the family home, then let everyone else know they can stop the search, Mrs. Navarro is fine."

Stacey waited with the woman until Abel and his little girl, along with his father, arrived to take Mrs. Navarro home.

They watched as Mr. Navarro gently shook his wife's shoulder. "Wake up, Carmela. Time to go home."

"Grammy, Grammy, you need to get up," Lupita called.

Obviously puzzled and disoriented, she shook her head and stared at those gathered around her. Speaking in Spanish, she asked her husband what was going on, and why she was in this strange place.

Lupita ran to her grandmother. The woman gathered the girl into her arms and started to cry.

■

Vince Aragon got the word that Mrs. Navarro had been found. He started on his regular patrol route when he received another call from the dispatcher. "Burglary in progress on the bluff." She gave the address. He turned on his lights but not the siren, in hopes he could catch the suspect before he got away.

The address turned out to be on a street he'd never gone down before. This was one was about four blocks from the houses with an ocean view, but these homes, with beautifully manicured lawns, were large and worth a lot of money. The two-story Moorish-style house had a tile roof and long narrow windows upstairs and down. The upstairs ones had small balconies with wrought iron railings. Aragon parked, leaped out of the car and ran up to the oval-shaped entry and tried the knob on the dark wooden door. It opened easily. With his gun out, he pushed the door open a crack. Stupid people, another unlocked door.

Two rifle shots rang out, followed by several thuds.

■

CHAPTER 7

VAUGHN SPOTTED A boy standing at the top of the circular staircase with a rifle pointed in Vaughn's direction. He raised his service revolver. His finger twitched on the trigger. "Put down the gun."

The boy didn't move.

"Do it now." Sweat beaded on Vaughn's forehead and he felt dampness under his arms.

A man dressed in black jeans and a black hooded sweatshirt sprawled across the bottom two steps and onto the white marble floor. Dark crimson blood pooled under his head. He didn't move.

Vaughn glanced back at the boy standing frozen, huge eyes staring.

Vaughn had come within seconds of shooting the kid. He wasn't a threat, and obviously, neither was the man. Breathing deeply, Vaughn tried calming himself. His hand holding the gun shook. He put it back into its holster.

Using a quieter voice, he said, "Son, put the rifle down on the floor, please." Vaughn waited until the boy did as instructed before stepping over to the body on the floor. Squatting, Vaughn touched two fingers to the man's carotid artery. No pulse.

He peered up at the boy again. He was no more than nine or ten years old, barefoot, in Spiderman pajamas. Blond hair stuck up in tufts all over his head. "Is he dead? I aimed for his legs. I wasn't trying to kill him." Talking fast, he sounded on the verge of tears.

Vaughn radioed in the situation and asked for an ambulance, though he knew it was too late. "Come on down here, son. Leave the rifle where it is."

Clinging to the wrought-iron banister, the youngster hurried down the stairs. When he reached the steps where the body lay, he jumped to avoid contact. He moved close to Vaughn.

"I'm Officer Aragon. What's your name?"

"Tommy. Tommy Jasper."

"Did you see anyone else with this guy?"

"No."

If there had been an accomplice, he'd be gone by now. In any case, Vaughn didn't want to leave the boy to look for one. That could be done once the detectives arrived.

"Will you tell me what happened, Tommy?" Vaughn glanced around. Near the entrance of what was probably the living room, a plasma TV was on the floor along with a DVD player, a bulging pillowcase and other household items.

Tommy still sounded scared. "I had a stomach ache and stayed home from school today. I was upstairs playing a video game when I heard noises down here. I crawled out and peeked through the railing and saw that guy there taking things out of the living room. My dad just bought that TV. There was no way I was going to let him get away with that."

"What did you do?"

"I snuck into my parents' room and called 911. The lady who answered told me to stay on the line and keep talking, but I was too scared. I dropped the phone on the bed. I didn't think you'd get here in time. I got the key to my dad's gun cabinet and took out his rifle. He keeps it loaded." He glanced up at Vaughn like he was going to be scolded.

Vaughn patted Tommy's shoulder. "I don't blame you. What did you do next?"

The wailing of approaching sirens grew louder.

"When I came back with the rifle, that guy," he turned toward the body on the floor, "was coming up the stairs. I was afraid what he might do to me so I shot him in the legs. He fell down and I guess he hit his head pretty hard."

"Have you ever shot a rifle before?" Vaughn asked.

"Sure. My dad and I shoot targets all the time."

"You did okay, Tommy. The burglar picked the wrong house this time."

Brakes squeaked outside and two pudgy EMTs in dark blue uniforms barreled through the door. “What have we got?”

Vaughn motioned toward the body. “D.O.A.”

While they were bending over the man, Detectives Milligan and Marshall entered the house. Vaughn briefly explained what he knew, his hand on the boy’s shoulder. “This is Tommy Jasper. Brave kid.” He hoped the two detectives wouldn’t notice how shaken he was.

“Hi, Tommy.” Milligan smiled at the boy. “Have you called this young man’s parents?”

“Not yet.”

“I’ll take care of it,” Marshall said. “Okay, Tommy. Why don’t you come over here with me.”

The boy moved with Marshall and away from the activity around the body.

The EMTs confirmed the man was dead. “Wasn’t from being shot. He hit his head on this marble floor and split his skull. Coroner will have to take this one.”

“I’ll call him,” Milligan said. “Thanks, guys.” He turned to Vaughn. “Have you determined where the burglar made his entry?”

“Not yet. I didn’t want to leave the kid alone or take him with me in case there was an accomplice on the scene.”

“I’ve got another job for you. How about scouting the neighborhood? See if you can find this guy’s vehicle. Maybe the neighbors noticed something.”

Vaughn was glad to get out of the house. He’d come way too close to shooting another kid. His heart still pounded too hard and he could feel the sweat pooling on his brow. He certainly didn’t want the detectives to see how he’d been affected.

A group of neighbors gathered across the street, no doubt attracted by all the unusual activity. Taking a deep breath in an effort to pull himself together, Vaughn used the sleeve of his uniform to wipe his forehead before marching across the street. “Excuse me, folks, but I need to ask you some questions.”

An elderly couple moved closer to him. The white haired woman introduced herself and asked, “Is Tommy okay? We know he didn’t go to school today.”

“Tommy’s just fine. How did you know he was home?”

“My wife and I like to eat our breakfast right beside our bay window,” the man said. "We enjoy watching what's going on in the neighborhood. We usually see Tommy walk to the bus stop every day soon after his mother and father leave for work. Today he didn't go."

"Did you see anything else out of the ordinary?" Vaughn asked.

The old couple stared at each other and shook their heads. "Not until you pulled up with your lights flashing."

A middle-aged stocky woman wearing a pink sweat suit said, "I heard gun shots."

No doubt everyone in the vicinity did. Vaughn asked her, "Did you see any unusual vehicles in the neighborhood this morning?"

"Actually, I did. I went shopping early and when I came home I noticed a black van driving down the street. I've never seen it before."

"Can you describe it for me?"

"I don't really know the names of the different kinds of cars. This was one of those delivery vans with no windows on the sides, a door in the back. It was really dirty. That's what made me notice. Most of the people around here have new cars and keep them clean."

"Which way was it going?" Vaughn asked.

She pointed to the north.

"Thanks folks, you've been very helpful." He re-crossed the street and began jogging in the direction the woman had indicated where she saw the van. He passed plush lawns and colorful flower gardens. Pausing at the corner, he peered down the street and spotted an alley that ran behind the houses on that block. Six-foot fences or brick walls protected the back yards. Each barrier had a cut-out spot for a trash bin.

About the middle of the alley, approximately the location of the Jaspers' home, he spotted a dirty black van. Since the van remained, the burglar had probably acted alone. When Vaughn reached it, he noted the trash bin had been pulled away from the inset just enough to create a step-up to climb over the back wall. Vaughn tried the back door of the van. It opened easily. The burglar was as dumb as the homeowners.

The van was half full of loot: TVs, computers, printers, video games.

He shut the door.

He returned to the house to tell the detectives what he'd found. The coroner had arrived as well as the boy's mother, a nice looking woman, though understandably upset.

When Vaughn walked in, she was hugging her son. "What do you mean, he'll have to go to the police station? Are you charging him with something? He was only trying to protect himself."

"Yes, ma'am, we certainly understand that. We aren't charging him with anything." Detective Milligan did his best to calm her. "We need him to go to the station to tell us exactly what happened for the police report. I can assure you it won't take long."

The woman was obviously suspicious. She didn't seem convinced her son was going to the police station for routine reasons. No doubt she'd seen too many police shows on TV. "Do I need to call our lawyer?"

Detective Marshall polished his bald spot. "No, ma'am. There's no need for a lawyer. Believe me, this really won't take long. It's merely a formality. It might be a good idea to call your husband. We'll be here awhile going over the crime scene."

The woman's voice rose an octave. "Crime scene?"

Again, Milligan stepped in. "Yes, ma'am. A burglary suspect died here. For everyone's sake, we need to make sure we've taken all the photographs we need for evidence."

"My husband's already on his way. I called him right after I was notified. This is so traumatic for my son. The sooner we can get this over with, the better."

Though Tommy had certainly been visibly shaken when Vaughn had first arrived, now he seemed to be reveling in the excitement.

The boy grasped his mother's hand. "It's okay, mom. I've never been inside the police station."

"Can we go now, ma'am?" Detective Milligan asked. "Might be a good idea if your son put on some shoes."

Mrs. Jasper's mouth dropped open. It was as though she was seeing her son for the first time. "Oh my goodness, Tommy, you're still in your pajamas. Detective, my son has been ill. He needs to put on some clothes before he goes anywhere."

Under his mother's direction, Tommy was properly dressed. Detective

Milligan drove the boy and his mother to the police station. The coroner took charge of the body, letting Detective Marshall know that it was obvious the burglar's death was caused by his head striking the marble floor, not the bullet wounds in the fleshy parts of his calf and thigh.

Vaughn was finally able to tell Detective Marshall what he'd found in the alley.

Mr. Jasper arrived, seemingly more horrified by the sight of his possessions piled in the entry to the living room than the dark pool of blood on the white marble floor. After he calmed down, Marshall asked Mr. Jasper to sit somewhere out of the way.

Vaughn left to find where the burglar had gained entrance, simple since the back door stood wide open. Another case of easy access. Photographs were taken. The rifle the boy discarded at the top of the stairs was logged in as evidence, much to Mr. Jasper's verbalized annoyance. He quieted after being assured it would be returned in a matter of days.

A tow truck was called to take the van to the impound yard.

Vaughn was released to go back to the station and write his incident report.

■

Gordon Butler had participated in the search for Abel Navarro's mother. After her safe return home, he resumed his regular patrol duty. He managed to hand out a couple of speeding tickets. He could always catch someone who'd just come off the freeway going too fast on the residential streets. While he was at the other end of town, the dispatcher reported a burglary in progress. Officer Aragon responded. Gordon felt a tug of envy. Seemed like the new guy got all the good calls.

For most of the afternoon, he cruised the residential area without incident. He decided to go back to the freeway exit when he spotted a fairly new Ford Focus weaving back and forth across an older residential street. He made a U-turn, turned on his light bar and siren.

The blue coupe bounced off one curb, careened across the street and bounced off the opposite one. It knocked over a curbside mailbox, breaking the support in two. The driver ignored the stop sign at the corner. The Ford continued on, weaving through the intersection.

The guy had to be drunk.

Gordon radioed in to the dispatcher, "I'm in pursuit going north on Pinon Avenue. Speed is about eight miles per hour." Pursuit was an odd word when he followed along at such a slow speed. He gave the license number to the dispatcher.

While on the wrong side of the road, the Ford bumped into the front end of a parked Chevy truck which didn't budge. The Ford finally came to a stop. "End of pursuit. Car crashed."

Gordon jumped out of his blue-and-white, and ran to the Ford. The window was open, and Gordon bent down to look inside.

A girl, not more than twelve or thirteen, stared back at him, defiance in her expression. "What do you want?" Her words slurred.

Alcohol vapors floated toward Gordon.

After the crazy driving, the fact she was under the influence, was no surprise. "Are you okay?" he asked.

"What do you care?" Her grin was crooked.

Though he knew she was too young to have one, Gordon asked, "May I see your driver's license, please?"

"Do I look like I have driver's license?" Big brown eyes gazed up at him with feigned innocence. Freckles dotted a turned-up nose.

"No, young lady, you don't, but what you do look is drunk."

"I'm too young to drink." She giggled.

"What's your name?"

"Not telling. You'll just call my parents." She pouted.

This was getting nowhere. "Let me see your arm."

She held her left hand up. Gordon cuffed her wrist to the steering wheel.

"What'd you do that for?" She began honking the horn with her other hand. People poured out of their homes.

Gordon radioed the station and told the dispatcher what was happening. "If Stacey Wilbur is around, see if she'll transport this juvenile into the station for me."

■

It took both Stacey and Gordon to drag the girl to the patrol car Stacey had driven to the scene.

The youngster pulled against them and hollered all the way. "Pigs." "Leggo, you're hurting me," accompanied by a slew of curse words. "Someone help me."

After a struggle, they managed to get her seat-belted and locked in the back. She began kicking the windows. "Lovely child," Stacey said. "I'll get her down to the station. You going to be able to handle the rest of the situation?"

Gordon felt his cheeks flame. Did she think he was incompetent? "Of course. If you can locate the owner of the car, send him or her over. If not, I'll call a tow truck. I'll find out who the owner of the Chevy is—probably one of the spectators."

"Okay, see you back at the station."

"Thanks, Stacey."

"You're welcome. By the way, have you been able to get Saturday off for the wedding?"

"Yes, I traded shifts with Aragon."

"Good. I'm glad you're going to be our best man, Gordon." Stacey waved when she got back into her police car with her noisy passenger.

■

Stacey struggled to get the girl out of the back seat of the blue-and-white. Every time she reached inside, feet flailed at her, and a barrage of swear words assaulted her ears.

Officer Aragon moved beside Stacey. "Wow, that is the worst blast of bad language I've heard since I left L.A. Maybe I can help." He peered into the car. "What do you know? That's a girl."

"Indeed, and she's also a drunk driver who managed to wreck what is probably her parents' car."

"My, my, Rocky Bluff certainly has its share of precocious kids."

The girl continued to shriek and curse as Vaughn held her legs to stop her kicking while Stacey released the seat belt. Together they hauled her out of the patrol car.

Aragon held one arm of the girl and Stacey the other as they carried her inside the station. She made so much noise, calling them names, people came out of offices to see what was going on.

"Where are we taking her?" Vaughn asked.

"Not sure. Be impossible to fingerprint her or take her picture while she's acting like this. I don't think putting her in lock-up is appropriate."

The girl stopped fighting them and became dead weight. Vaughn and Stacey paused. He squinted at the kid. "She passed out."

Stacey agreed. "I think she needs to go to the hospital. She may have alcohol poisoning."

One of the dispatchers was seated at the table drinking coffee as Vaughn carried the limp body of the girl and deposited her on a couch. She immediately curled up, a peaceful grin on what was actually a pretty face.

The dispatcher, a heavy set woman with dark graying hair pulled into a pony tail said, "Ah, must be the juvenile drunk driver. You'll be happy to know her mother is on the way to pick her up."

"Call her back," Stacey said. "We're going to send her to the hospital. Tell the mom I'll meet her there."

"Juvenile hall might be more appropriate than the hospital." Vaughn turned toward the door.

She ignored his remark. "Thanks for helping me. I'd have had a difficult time getting her inside without your assistance."

Vaughn paused while Stacey called for an ambulance. "No problem."

When Stacey knew the paramedics were on the way, she added, "I also want to thank you for trading shifts with Butler so he can be in my wedding."

"No problem. By the way, what about tomorrow morning? Still want to try for that beach pervert?"

Stacey grinned. "Why not? We ought to give it one more shot."

CHAPTER 8

WHAT HAPPENED WITH Abel's mother emphasized the seriousness of her problem for Abel's father. When they arrived at the house, he guided her into their bedroom telling her to take a shower and get dressed.

Abel could hear his mother's protests. "But Abel and Lupita are here. I should make them something to eat."

Sounding firm but caring, his father said. "I'll take care of them. You need to get dressed." Next came the sound of the shower.

Lupita took hold of Abel's hand. "Is something wrong with Grandma?" Worry showed on her sweet face.

Abel scooped his daughter into his arms and kissed her. "Grandma's confused. She'll be better after she has her shower."

"I love Grandma."

"I know you do, honey. And she loves you."

"Maybe I can help her." She looked at Abel like she expected him to fix her grandmother.

"Just keep loving her." Abel blinked back the tears that stung his eyes.

His father came back into the room. "She seems to be better, acting more like her old self." He shrugged. "She shooed me out of the bathroom. Told me she had a lot to do today and for me to stay out of her way."

"What can I do to help, Pop?"

Pressing his lips together and shaking his head, his father said, "I wish I knew. I have to get Carmela to the doctor fast. Where is that paper with the appointment?"

Abel picked it up from the desk and handed it to his father.

"I've never been as scared as I was today when we could not find Carmela. All sorts of horrible thoughts ran through my head. What will I do without my Carmela?"

Abel couldn't think of anything reassuring to say, so he put his hand on his father's shoulder and squeezed. "If you don't need me for anything else, I think I better take Lupita home."

Lupita leaned away from her father and kissed her grandpa. "Love you. Tell Grandma I love her too."

Abel's father touched Lupita's cheek with the back of his hand. "We both love you so much, little one."

"Call me if you need anything, Pop."

His father nodded and smiled briefly. He glanced at the paper with the appointment information. He folded it and stuck it into his shirt pocked and headed back toward the bedroom and his wife.

How had his father become so old and tiny without Abel noticing? He shook his head. He always thought both of his parents were strong and able to face whatever came along with courage. Though his mother had always seemed to be the one running things, Abel and his brothers knew that Pop ruled the household and family. Carmela fussed a lot, and criticized her daughters-in-law, but if she stepped too far out-of-bounds, their father could rein her in with a single look.

Carrying Lupita, her arms wrapped around him, Abel left his parents' home.

■

Aragon wrote his report about the robbery suspect shot by the kid and the suspect's van found in the alley behind the house. He'd just completed the paperwork, when the boy and his family left to be immediately surrounded by news people eager to learn more.

■

Stacey followed the ambulance to the hospital. Already hooked up to an IV, the girl was moved into one of the cubicles in the emergency room. Stacey stood in the corridor while a nurse checked vital signs and took blood which would be checked for the alcohol level and routine lab work done.

The arrival of the young drunk driver's mother was apparent by her screaming at the top of her lungs, "Where's my child? What's wrong with her?"

Stacey stepped toward the receiving area and told the receptionist to open the door to let the woman inside the restricted area. "Ma'am, please calm down. I'm Officer Wilbur. I had your daughter brought to the hospital."

The woman wore a gray pants suit, a blouse with ruffles, and a tag on the lapel of her jacket with the logo of a local real estate company and the name Miranda Pharr. She stomped toward Stacey, her high heels staccato on the tile floor. Her shoulder-length dark brown hair swirled around a face that might have been attractive if it wasn't so contorted with fury. "Don't you tell me to calm down. I was told my daughter was in an accident. No one said she was injured. Why is she here?"

"Mrs. Pharr, listen please. Your daughter wasn't hurt. Another officer spotted her driving erratically and tried to pull her over. She was in your car and ran into someone else's."

Her expression changed immediately. "If she wasn't injured why was she brought to the hospital? Are you people crazy? You scared me half to death."

"Please, hear me out. Then I'll take you to your daughter. Mrs. Pharr, you daughter not only drove your car, she did so while intoxicated."

"That's impossible. She doesn't have a driver's license. She doesn't even know how to drive. And where did she get alcohol?"

"That I don't know. What I do know is she's still drunk. She passed out at the police station and that's why I decided she should be transported to the hospital for an examination."

"I'm finding all this hard to believe. Are you sure it's my daughter you're talking about?" Mrs. Pharr frowned and shook her head.

"Yes, ma'am. Your name is on the vehicle's registration. She wouldn't tell us her name, but she looks like she's about twelve or thirteen, has brown eyes and hair."

Once again Mrs. Pharr's expression changed, this time from disbelief to shock. "That does sound like my daughter." Her voice tinged with resignation, she continued, "Carrie is supposed to be in school. In fact, I planned to pick her up later. I left the car home because one of my colleagues drove me to work today. We were both showing houses on the bluff. In fact, she's waiting for me outside. What am I going to do without a car?"

"If it's any consolation, Carrie wasn't driving very fast when she had her accident. I doubt if there's a lot of damage. Your car is probably still drivable. The officer who witnessed the accident is still at the scene. After you find out about your daughter's condition and make a decision about what should be done about her, you'll need to go there."

Mrs. Pharr frowned. "I don't know what you plan to do, but I'm grounding her for the rest of her life."

"Of course, she could go to juvenile hall, but I don't think that's the best plan. If you're willing to take her home and deal with her and the owner of the other car, that would probably be best. You do have insurance, don't you?"

"Juvenile hall? No, please, I don't want her there. I don't know what got into her, but I promise nothing like this will ever happen again. Yes, I do have insurance. Oh, heavens, my rates will sky-rocket after this."

Stacey nodded, knowing full well that a mother couldn't keep a promise that her child would never get in trouble again. But a juvenile hall experience might make things worse. To be perfectly honest, Stacey didn't really want to go to the trouble of finding out if the hall had room for the girl and all the paperwork that went along with it. Giving custody of the youngster to her mother seemed like the best solution for this first offense.

Stacey escorted Mrs. Pharr to the cubicle where Carrie still lay curled up.

A doctor stood by the side of the girl's bed.

Mrs. Pharr gasped, her hand to her mouth. "Oh, heavens, it is Carrie. I kept hoping it might have been someone else."

"Are you the mother?" the doctor asked.

Mrs. Pharr nodded, blinking back tears.

"We've done some blood tests and a urine test. We're going to keep monitoring her. She won't be going anywhere until she's awake enough to answer questions intelligibly and her blood alcohol level is under .2."

"She looks so pitiful. Is she going to be all right? "

"Oh yes. She might not feel like doing much for awhile, but that's probably a good thing."

"This is so humiliating. I can't believe Carrie actually did this. She's never caused me a bit of trouble before."

Stacey doubted the accuracy of the Mrs. Pharr's statement.

The doctor spoke again. "If this was her first time drinking, it probably didn't take much alcohol to put her in this condition."

"How long do you think you'll keep her?" Stacey asked.

"A couple of hours." The doctor paid little attention to the conversation going on between Stacey and Mrs. Pharr.

Turning to the mother, Stacey said, "You ought to go see about your car before the officer on the scene has it towed. If that happens you'll have that expense on top of everything else."

"Oh, goodness. I don't need that. Will it be okay for me to leave? Doctor, are you sure Carrie is going to be okay?"

The doctor didn't bother to look up from the chart he wrote on. "Yes, I'm sure."

Stacey handed Mrs. Pharr her card. "I've written the address on the back where you'll find your car. I'll let Officer Butler know you're coming. You can give your insurance company a call from there, talk to the owner of the other car, and decide what you want to do. Good luck with Carrie. Hope I don't see either of you again under similar circumstances."

Stacey could tell Mrs. Pharr was indecisive. She wanted to stay with her daughter, but she also wanted to take care of her car situation. The car won out.

■

That evening, after tucking Davey into bed, Stacey agreed to meet Doug at the café for coffee. She entered to find him waiting in their favorite back booth. When she walked in he grinned broadly, his dimple deepening.

He slid out and embraced her, kissing her cheek. "I can't stand not seeing you more often."

"Me too. But sweetheart, it won't be much longer. Our wedding is only a couple of days away."

The waitress headed in their direction with a coffee pot.

Stacey slid into the booth across from Doug knowing that he'd hoped she'd sit next to him. "I really can't stay long."

The waitress poured coffee into the cup in front of Stacey. Doug reached across the table and took her hand. "It's driving me crazy only getting glimpses of you at work and not having any time alone together."

"Actually you should feel lucky we're not doing all the usual things that go along with a wedding."

"Like what?"

"The ceremony is simple and we don't need a rehearsal, so no rehearsal dinner to go along with that."

"Yeah, I vaguely remember something like that with my first wedding."

"Usually the husband's family pays for that," Stacey teased.

"Except for my kids, I don't have any family." Doug's parents died several years ago. "I'd be stuck footing the bill."

"Consider yourself blessed as I do that the church ladies are providing the food for the reception and taking care of the decorations. Like I promised, we really are having a small wedding."

"It can't come too soon for me." He rubbed her ankle with his toe.

Stacey smiled at his attempt to change her mind. "I feel the same way. Once Saturday afternoon arrives, our lives will be changed forever. We'll be husband and wife."

"I'm counting the minutes." He picked up her hand, massaging it between his own much larger, strong hands.

Stacey lifted an eyebrow. "You do remember that you're going to have a six-year old boy to contend with, right?"

"Davey will be a welcome replacement for Gordon Butler. Your son couldn't possibly manage to interrupt as many romantic moments as my soon-to-be former roommate."

"Don't be too sure about that, sweetheart. Davey is used to having his mommy all to himself. Plus, he's pretty excited about having you for his new daddy."

"I remember what it was like with my own kids." Doug released Stacey's hand and leaned against the back of the booth. He grinned. "We did have a few embarrassing moments. That's why I installed a lock on my bedroom door."

"I've had a little talk with Davey about how after you and I are married we need time to ourselves." She smiled. "His answer was, 'I know. For all that smooching stuff.'"

"That's exactly what I'm missing, all that smooching stuff." Doug leaned forward again. "Are you positive you can't stop by my house for a bit? I'm sure I could chase Gordon off for awhile—appeal to his romantic side." He winked at her.

"As much as I'd like to, I really can't. I have to get up early tomorrow."

A line deepened across Doug's forehead. "Why? Is something going on I don't know about?"

"Aragon and I are hitting the beach again on the off chance that the pervert didn't hear the public safety announcement. I'd love to catch this guy and put him out of commission." Stacey could tell by the expression on Doug's face he wasn't thrilled with the prospect of her playing decoy again. At least he had the good sense not to say anything about it—or she hoped he did. Surprisingly, he changed the subject.

"What's your impression of Aragon?" Doug asked. "You've probably spent as much time with him as anyone."

"He's okay. Seems to be a good guy. Don't think he's particularly happy, but he likes to be on the job."

"Yeah, heard he's pulling another double shift tonight with Zachary, keeping the peace at the angel sighting downtown."

"Barbara Strickland told me I should take Davey to see it. Have you any idea what's causing the apparition?"

"If it's not a hoax, it's got to be a reflection of some sort."

"No matter what it is, if seeing an angel in a window makes people happy I don't suppose there's any harm in it. No one's making money off it, are they?"

"I understand a taco truck set up business on the corner." Doug drank some of his coffee.

"Smart. Why not take advantage of the crowd. Mom said if the reflection is still there after the wedding she'd like to see it. Right now, we're all too busy." Stacey realized she hadn't even touched her coffee and took a sip. Lukewarm. She glanced at her watch. "I've really got to get home." She stood before Doug could protest.

"I'll walk you out." He tossed a five dollar bill on the table. With his hand on her waist, he followed her past the other booths and out to her car.

Glancing down the street, she was shocked to see how many people had gathered on the sidewalk nearly two blocks away. "My goodness. Look at that.

There really is a crowd. I had no idea an angel sighting could draw so many people."

Doug put his arms around her and drew her close. "One of these days, someone will figure out what's causing it and the whole thing will be over."

She stood on tiptoe and held her face toward his. She loved the way he felt as she pressed against him, the way he smelled, his aftershave, his coffee breath.

He didn't need more of an invitation to kiss her.

For only a moment she enjoyed his arms tightening around her, his lips on hers, his slightly salty taste, the urgency of his kiss, the quickening of his breath.

Gently pushing him away, she said, "I don't want to, but I have to go."

"You're killing me." He released her, his eyes yearning.

"I know." She hurried to the driver's side of her car. It wouldn't take much urging on his part to change her mind about going home. "Love you." She blew him a kiss, unlocked the door and climbed in.

He slapped the top of her VW. "Love you too. Be careful tomorrow."

■

As Stacey drove off and Doug headed back to his vehicle, Vaughn Aragon and Felix Zachary had already stationed themselves in the median of Valley Boulevard.

"Man, there are more people here than last night," Vaughn said. Knowing what the parking would be like, he'd come early and positioned his squad car close to the store with the fascinating front window. Zachary hadn't been so fortunate. He'd parked his blue-and-white in a yellow zone a block-and-a-half away.

"Yeah, the word's been spreading. Didn't know we had so many religious people in Rocky Bluff."

"Probably most of 'em are curious more than religious. They aren't all from this town, heard some people say they'd come up from Ventura and another bunch came down from Santa Barbara."

"Long as they behave themselves, I don't care how many come to see the angel."

"Did you get a chance to eat?" Vaughn asked.

"Oh sure. I always eat at home before I come to work. What about you? I know you're working a double shift again."

"Yeah. I came early and the taco truck had already set up for business. Had two really good burritos."

"I suppose we ought to check and see if they have a business license."

"Already did, though after I bit into my food, I wouldn't have cared whether they did or not. The license is on display inside the truck. Probably not legal for them to be set up in the parking lot like that—but who cares."

"As long as it keeps people happy, I agree. Heard you had some excitement today."

"You mean the kid shooting the burglar? From the looks of what the dead guy had in the back of his van, he's the one responsible for the rash of home burglaries we've had. That boy did us a favor."

While keeping an eye on the ever-growing crowd, the men continued to discuss different cases they'd been on in the past; and joked about Gordon Butler's talent for trouble.

The sound level didn't reflect the size of the crowd. Even while jostling against one another for a better viewing spot, an oddly reverent attitude settled over the people keeping them calm and quiet as they each managed to get a glimpse of the image that resembled a large angel. People continued to snap pictures from cameras and cell phones. They spoke to one another in subdued tones.

"I wouldn't be a bit surprised if someone broke out in a hymn," Felix said.

Vaughn snickered. "*Amazing Grace* might be appropriate."

"Wonder how long they'll keep coming to look at this thing."

"Until someone figures out what's causing it or something more exciting comes along. It's okay by me, haven't got anything better to do with my evenings. Might as well make some extra money." It wouldn't do to mention what a hard time he had going to sleep when he finally returned to his crummy motel room. Light filtered through the frayed drapes. A trained rattled by ever time he started to nod off. When he did sleep, the kid he'd shot in L.A. visited him in horrifying nightmares. No one needed to know that much about him.

■

CHAPTER 9

COLORED LIGHTS FILTERED through the multi-paned windows of the enclosed porch at the front of Doug's Victorian. Gordon Butler must still be up watching TV. Doug passed through the empty porch which used to hold all sorts of potted plants that left along with Kerrie and the kids. He suspected once Stacey and her son moved in, the porch would be a great place for any overflow of Davey's toys. He'd also thought of buying an old-fashioned porch swing for Stacey and him to spend some of their leisure time—if they had any.

When Doug entered the house, he found Gordon embedded in the cushions of the overstuffed couch, his stocking feet propped on the coffee table. Without glancing away from the basketball game on TV, he said, "Hey, thought you had a date with Stacey this evening."

"We saw each other, had some coffee. Wasn't much of a date." Doug tossed his keys on the dining room table.

"Good thing you two are getting married. Looks like that's going to be the only way you'll be able to spend more time together."

"I sure hope it works out that way. All Stacey can think about right now is the wedding." Doug plopped down on the far end of the couch. "You are going to have all your things packed and ready to move once we've tied the knot, right?"

"It won't take long. I haven't got that much. Some of my stuff is still in boxes from when I was supposed to rent a room from that little old lady who died."

Doug nodded. They watched the game for a few minutes without talking. Finally, he asked, "Anything exciting happen on your shift?"

Gordon told him about the drunk teenager. "Stacey came to my rescue and took the girl to the police station. I'm surprised she didn't tell you about it."

"I heard something about it at the station. We ought to call you Joe Btfsplk."

Frowning, Gordon turned his head toward Doug. "Joe who?"

"Didn't you ever hear of the comic book character Li'l Abner?"

"Yeah, I guess."

From the puzzled expression on his face, Doug guessed though Gordon had probably heard the name, he didn't know much more.

Doug hadn't thought about the comic strip or the characters for years, but Gordon certainly did have a resemblance to Joe Btfsplk. "When I was a kid, my dad read his precious collector copies of Li'l Abner comics to me. I knew all about him and his buddies." Doug grinned, thinking about his dad. "One of the characters called Joe Btfsplk was jinxed. A dark cloud traveled over his head. If anything bad was going to happen, it always happened to him."

Gordon jerked back. "Are you saying I'm jinxed?"

"Not exactly. If anything unusual is going to happen, it's a safe bet you'll be the one who gets the call."

"I can't help it if oddball things happen while I'm on duty." Gordon's face turned bright red.

"Now don't get upset, buddy. You've got to admit, the three years you've been a cop have been filled with the unusual. Not everyone wrecks two police cars, one of them brand new, during the first few weeks on the job."

"Aw, Doug. Aren't you ever going to let me forget that?"

"Kind of hard to forget stuff like that." Doug grinned at him.

Gordon laughed. "Wish you would." He turned toward Doug, his expression serious. "You aren't going to tell anyone else about this Joe Bispick character, are you?"

"It's Joe Btfsplk. Nope, in the first place no one would get it, or even be able to pronounce the name."

"Thanks, I guess." Gordon turned back to the TV, his lower lip jutted out.

Doug hadn't meant to make Gordon uncomfortable. "Sorry for teasing you. Sometimes I can't help myself." He didn't add that Gordon left himself wide open for teasing. "You've been a good friend." And he had. After Doug's wife left, Gordon rented one of the empty upstairs bedrooms. It was nice to come home to a friend instead of an empty house. When Doug and Stacey decided to get married, they also realized the old Victorian needed a fresh coat of paint. After Stacey and he picked out the colors, Gordon rolled on the new paint right beside them.

Doug squeezed Gordon's shoulder. "I'm glad you're going to be my best man." He headed toward the stairs. "Think I'll hit the sack. Hope your team wins."

■

When Abel crawled into bed, Maria woke and snuggled against him. "Did you get your mom settled?"

"After she took her shower and got dressed, she seemed more normal."

"How's your dad?"

"I'm really worried about him too. All of a sudden, he seems so tiny and frail."

"It's always a horrible shock for a man or woman to learn their life partner has any terrible disease. Alzheimer's is even harder to come to terms with, knowing eventually the one you love won't even know who you are."

"It's worse to learn your mother has it."

"I know." Maria smoothed Abel's hair back from his forehead and she kissed him. "She'll be better once she's on medication."

"Sure hope you're right."

"I am. Try to sleep now."

Often, when he climbed into bed after his shift and Maria woke, they made love. He had no desire tonight. She seemed to sense that and cuddled against him in a soothing manner rather than a seductive one. Her warmth and the softness of her body stirred nothing in him. The events of the day left him unsettled and emotionally drained.

Drifting off, that wriggling worm in the back of his brain told him that he'd forgotten to do or take care of something important.

■

Thick fog rolled in from the ocean obliterating from view everything farther than ten yards away. Because of this, Stacey met Aragon a little after seven a.m. near where he'd tucked his police car at the end of a long driveway next to an empty house. No one could see his vehicle unless they peered directly down the drive.

Aragon had been the first to arrive. Stacey parked her yellow bug in front of the house and walked to where he leaned against his car. "Hey, Aragon, ready for our big day?"

"Yeah, sure. Same deal as before?" He had dark circles under his eyes.

"Big night?" Stacey asked.

"Ha. Haven't had a big night since I arrived in this burg. Worked a double shift."

"Yeah, I heard. What's it like?"

He shrugged. "Crowd control. Making sure things didn't get out of hand while everyone's staring at that angel in the window."

"Have you seen it?"

"Yeah. Some trick with the lighting."

"What does it look like?"

"An angel I suppose, though it's not like any angel I've ever seen."

"You've seen a lot of angels?"

His face flushed. "You know what I mean. Doesn't look like pictures of angels on Christmas cards and the like."

"Sorry. I was just kidding you. I'd like to see it, but I've been too busy with my wedding plans. Hey, thanks again for switching days off with Gordon so he can be in the wedding."

"No problem." Aragon glanced at his watch. "We should get going on the off-chance our suspect is going to do his thing this morning."

"You're right. See you in a bit. I'm going to start off at the usual place and jog slowly all the way down to the pier and back again."

■

Once she'd parked her bug in the sandy turn-around at the end of the street, she did a few stretches. Why not do everything she'd usually do before going on a run in case their suspect had spotted her?

Though the sun was up, it couldn't seem to break through the thick mist swirling around the beach. Coming over the sand dune, at first, though she could hear the breakers, she couldn't see the ocean. It wasn't until she'd nearly reached the part of the sand dampened by the waves swirling into shore that the gray sea came into view. Perfect atmosphere for any kind of criminal activity. She shivered though not really cold.

Stacey figured their suspect had seen or heard the public service announcements and wouldn't show, they had to give it a try in case he'd missed it or, perhaps, had the audacity to show up anyway. Maybe he thought if any jogger was brave enough to appear despite the warning, he could be too. Certainly, Stacey would never see anyone until he was right in front—or in back of her.

She started her run down the beach, hoping the fog would lift.

Hope wasn't enough. If anything the mist swirled thicker and her vision reduced to a few feet ahead. She knew Aragon couldn't possibly spot her from his vantage point on the sand dune—nor would she be able to see the suspect until he was right upon her—if he did show up.

Under the circumstances, this might not be such a good idea.

The salty air felt much damper than the day before. As she ran on the damp sand, particles she kicked up pricked her ankles and calves. She could hear the plaintive cries of the seagulls, but couldn't see them.

Squinting, she couldn't see the expensive seafood restaurant, but felt must be near it. This was one of the places a victim had reported an encounter with the psycho. Without incident, she jogged on past, the structure appearing out of the mist and disappearing behind her.

Minutes later she thought she spotted the old pier jutting through the fog, but it was nothing more than a dark blur on the horizon. Time to turn around.

On the way back, Stacey began thinking about her coming wedding. One more day until she'd be Mrs. Doug Milligan. Stacey's heart raced every time she thought about it. A comforting warmth enveloped her. At first she'd had misgivings about marrying again, especially to another cop, but all doubt had ultimately dissipated.

Whenever she thought about Doug or spent time with him, she knew she'd found the man she wanted to spend the rest of her life with. She had no illusions about him being perfect. No one was. As much as she'd loved her first husband, it didn't take long after they'd become husband and wife to learn they both had flaws. Loving one another meant they overlooked those flaws and rejoiced in the intimacy and good times together, and worked their way through the bad ones.

The first time she'd married her high school sweetheart. Davey arrived a year later. Having a good marriage and a child was wonderful until a drunk driver T-boned her husband's car in an intersection. He was pronounced dead at the scene. For a long time she doubted she'd ever again find the happiness she had with Davey's father.

Euphoria enveloped her. The same feeling she often experienced while running, only today thoughts of her impending wedding enhanced what she felt.

■

Vaughn Aragon couldn't see a damn thing through the thick fog. He scrubbed at his eyes, knowing that wouldn't help, but he had to try something. He wouldn't be able to see Stacey when she jogged past, or anyone else for that matter, including the suspect, should he appear.

He couldn't rely on his ears either. The crashing waves drowned everything else out. He decided to time how long he remembered it took her to jog past where he waited last time, then move closer to the water's edge. Why hadn't he suggested wearing civilian clothes so he wouldn't be quite so visible in his dark uniform?

Visible? Ha, nothing was visible in this pea soup. Crazy for them to even be out here. Too late now though, Stacey was out there committed to the plan. After hoping for the suspect to turn up, now he changed his mind. This would not be a good time for the bad guy to make an appearance. Circumstances were all in the suspect's favor.

If the guy did show up, Vaughn hoped Stacey would holler loud enough for him to hear her.

CHAPTER 10

STACEY'S SENSES WARNED her before she saw or heard anything. She could smell the salt air and the underlying scent of sea weed. The first new thing she noticed was a sharp citrus scent over a musky odor. Not a pleasant musk, but dank and nasty. She wondered if something had died on the beach.

A dark shape thrust through the fog, as if a curtain abruptly parted.

Stacey halted. She didn't have to pretend to be surprised.

A man, a stocking cap pulled down over his eyebrows, leered at her. What she noted first was that he was white, probably five-eleven, with a dark overcoat wrapped around his body.

His big hands yanked open the coat. A large erection immediately drew her attention. It was connected to a plump, pinkish body, sparsely covered with wiry brown hair and dark moles scattered here and there.

"Hey baby," the man cooed, revealing a surprisingly healthy and white set of teeth.

He wasn't a vagrant or a homeless person.

Thrusting himself towards her, he said, "Do you like what I have for you?" The rank musty smell billowed up from him in waves.

"For heaven's sake, mister, cover up," she said loudly. She hoped Aragon had witnessed what was happening, or at least heard what she said.

Her matter of fact comment stunned the pervert for a moment, but it didn't take long for him to recover and reach for her.

Stacey took a step forward and grabbed his outthrust wrist. Before he had time to react, she hooked her leg around his, flipped him over and knocked him down. She knelt on his back.

"What do you think you're doing?" The man's protest was muffled by the sand his face was buried in.

"Police officer. You're under arrest for indecent exposure."

"What?"

The man started to thrash around, kicking his legs, sending sand flying. Stacey already had her flexible cuffs out and one fastened around a wrist. She nearly had the other one on when the man arched his back and struggled against her.

At the top of her lungs, she hollered, "Aragon, I need you." And to the man lurching beneath her, "Settle down. Stop your wiggling."

It only took a minute before she felt and heard Aragon pounding across the sand toward her. "Sorry, I couldn't see a thing, but I was right over there." He pointed to what she supposed was a nearby dune, though not visible through the fog.

Aragon took a look at the man Stacey had pinned to the sand "Well, well, well, who have we got here?"

He checked the cuffs before hauling the guy to his feet. "Good work, Wilbur, I'm impressed. You nailed the pervert." And to the man, "Guess you're about the only one who didn't pay attention to the warning about staying off the beach."

The suspect spat sand from his mouth. "I don't know what you're talking about. I didn't do anything. This is outrageous."

"Sure, and you just happened to forget your clothes this morning before you went out for a stroll."

The man bellowed, "You'll be hearing from my lawyer."

"I'm sure we will." Aragon held the guy by his wrists and pushed him toward the sand dune. "Get moving."

"You haven't read me my rights."

"Don't have to until we're ready to question you. Don't worry, we'll do everything by the book once we get you into to the station."

"I'll come with you and make sure he gets settled in your car. If you don't mind, you can drop me off by my bug before you take him in."

"Sure. You're coming in too, aren't you?"

"Of course. I want to hear what he has to say for himself."

■

At the station, the suspect had his mug shot and fingerprints taken, but by then he clamed up. After his rights were read, he wouldn't even give his name, but continued to demand his lawyer be called. He had no ID or other personal items except a set of car keys in the pocket of his overcoat. He was tucked in a holding cell until his lawyer arrived. No chance of questioning him until then.

Once Stacey had the opportunity to see the man without the stocking cap, she realized he looked familiar. She knew she'd seen him somewhere before, but couldn't remember where. If she could get the disgusting image of his naked body out of her mind, she might be able to place who he was. His blondish hair had been recently cut and his pink cheeks were clean-shaven. Dressed properly, he'd look like any other business man. In fact, except for the fact he didn't have anything on except his overcoat, he wasn't what anyone would have expected to be a weenie-wagger.

She'd been thinking about him while heading down the hall to her computer and her desk, when it dawned on her. "That's it. I know who he is," she cried out to no one in particular.

Heads poked out from various doors, but Aragon who walked behind her was the one who asked, "Who?"

"One of our esteemed councilmen, good old Winston Blandly."

She knew this information made the arrest something Doug would want to be in on and hurried toward the office he shared with Detective Frank Marshall.

Both detectives came out of their office and headed toward her. Chewing gum as usual, Frank asked, "What's all the ruckus about?"

"Aragon and I caught the flasher and brought him in. Turns out our guilty party is none other than the esteemed Winston Blandly."

Doug reached Stacey first. "Councilman Blandly? What do you know! We'll have to handle this one carefully. Does the chief know about this yet?"

"I don't think so." Stacey turned and the trio headed back the way she'd come.

"Is his lawyer here?"

"No, but he's been called."

"I'll let Chief McKenzie know who's been arrested. I'm sure he'll want to be in on the questioning." Frank headed toward the chief's office and stepped inside.

■

Fingerprints proved Stacey to be correct. Besides being a Rocky Bluff Councilman, Blandly was one of the biggest opponents to any raise in police salaries or hiring more personnel or any other expenditure for the department. Even more interesting was the fact that he owned one of the biggest construction companies in the area and had been one of the loudest voices pushing for the city to condemn the old beachfront cottages and tear them down to make way for the proposed new development of condos and more expensive beach housing. No doubt he'd already paved the way for his construction company to do the building.

"What on earth would possess a man like Blandly to do something so disgusting?" Stacey asked Doug. "Surely he didn't think he could get away with it forever."

"The man's sick in the head. Perverted. We both know he has an inflated ego and probably thought he could do what he wanted no matter how disgusting or evil and get away with it. He doesn't have any respect for our department. I wouldn't be a bit surprised if he doesn't believe he's going to get out of this with little more than a fine and a slap on his wrist."

"Surely, he'll be charged with indecent exposure and lewd behavior. He was caught in the act by me—a police officer. Even if he pleads not guilty, we'll be able to get the other women he accosted to identify and testify against him."

"I agree that's how it should go, but you know as well as I do that sometimes things don't work out the way they should."

■

Ryan Strickland heard about the arrest and knew he'd be busy. Once the news got out about the arrest of the man who'd been exposing himself to women jogging on the beach, the station would be crawling with news people. The fact that the accused was a respected member of the community and an elected official would make it a hot item. No doubt this delectable news would even bring media from the larger cities.

It was important for Ryan to gather all the facts before preparing a list of the key information to give out. He'd learned over the years to be honest in his reporting to the press because anything he said could and would be used as a quote. No matter how aggravating the reporters were, he had trained himself to always be gracious.

He'd need time to wade through the reports, learn what the evidence was and talk to the primary parties. In this instance that was Officers Wilbur and Aragon.

Ryan found Stacey at her desk, still wearing her jogging clothes, her short hair windblown. He grinned at her. She looked more like a teenager then an undercover cop. "Hey, Stacey, hear you caught the guy exposing himself on the beach. Have you got time to talk to me about it?"

"Sure. I just finished filing my report. If you want, I'll print a copy for you."

"That would be great."

While they waited for the report, Ryan asked, "Did you recognize Councilman Blandly right away?"

Stacey shook her head. "The fog was horrible along the beach. I didn't even notice him until he popped up right in front of me. He whipped open his long overcoat and exposed himself in all his disgusting glory. I didn't even get a good look at his face until we brought him in to be processed. Even then, it took me a while to remember where I'd seen him before. After all, the few times he'd crossed my path he always had his pants on."

Ryan chuckled. "I imagine it was a bit of a shock when you realized who he is. I know I'll be asked this, how many times did you jog on the beach before he approached you?"

"This was only the second time. Aragon and I thought whoever was doing this would be scared off by your public service announcements. Guess he didn't hear them."

"I never did like that arrogant s.o.b. He always looked down his nose at me and any other law enforcement officer like we were lesser beings. Wouldn't be a bit surprised if we don't find something buried deep in his past. I doubt this is the first time he's been in trouble for this kind of perverted behavior."

"Doug and Frank are working on that now while waiting for Blandly's lawyer to show up."

"Did he physically resist you?" Ryan asked.

"Nope. I think he was too shocked by my reaction. Everyone else he's accosted ran off and I suppose he expected me to do the same. I had him down and cuffed before he had time to do much of anything."

Ryan couldn't help laughing again. The thought of this pompous windbag being taken down by tiny Stacey Wilbur warmed his heart. He'd have to control his feelings when he talked to the press. "Wish I could have seen his face."

"You wouldn't have seen much, it was buried in the sand." Stacey handed him the three pages of her printed report. "If you need anything else, just holler. By the way, how're Barbara and the boys?"

"She's really excited about the angel in the furniture store window. She and the boys have been out there every night. She believes it's a sign from God."

"Have you seen it?"

"Of course. She dragged me out there the first night she went."

"What do you think?"

"I must admit it's impressive, definitely looks like an angel, though not what I'd expected an angel to look like. Quite an attraction, drawing a huge crowd every night."

"You know, Ryan, it might really be a sign from God."

He studied her face to see if she was kidding him, but she looked serious. "Yeah, I suppose. Thanks for this." He lifted the report.

"You're welcome."

He turned to leave, but before he could get out the door, Stacey added, "Don't forget about my wedding on Saturday."

"Don't worry, we'll be there. Barbara has a big red circle around the date on the calendar in our kitchen."

■

Stacey wondered if she had time to go home and change clothes. She'd neglected to bring another set to put into her locker. The thought of talking to Blandly's lawyer in her jogging outfit didn't appeal to her and knew it wouldn't make much of an impression on him. She also wanted to get her engagement ring back on her finger where it belonged.

She walked back toward Doug's office, hoping he'd be there. She knocked and stepped inside. Frank glanced up from his computer, Doug's chair was empty.

"Hey, Stacey. What can I do for you?" As usual Frank was chomping on gum.

"I was hoping to find Doug, but you can probably answer my question."

"Doug's in front waiting for Blandly's lawyer. He and the chief want to be there when the lawyer arrives. Excellent report, by the way. Aragon's too. You certainly have the goods on this guy."

"Do you have any idea when the lawyer's going to get here? I'm pretty sure he'll want to talk to me too and I'd like to go home and change clothes before that happens."

"Nope, haven't heard. I suspect the lawyer's not thrilled. Probably dragging his feet. You got time, I'm sure. If anyone asks for you, I'll let them know where you've gone."

"Thanks, Frank. Don't forget the wedding on Saturday."

"Not to worry. I'm looking forward to this big event myself. Doug's driving me crazy with all his moaning and groaning about never getting to see you."

■

A disturbance in the waiting area drew everyone's attention. Doug turned to Chief McKenzie. "I'll see what's going on."

A woman shouted, "I have every right to go inside and see my husband. You let me in or I'll have your job."

Doug peeked into the receptionist section and mouthed, "The councilman's wife?"

The middle-aged woman at the desk nodded and turned back to the window. "I'm sorry ma'am, but you'll have to wait until I can get someone to come out and talk to you."

The woman continued to screech and make threats. Doug returned to the chief who stood outside his office. "It's Mrs. Blandly. Do you want me to speak with her?"

"Yes, please. But under no circumstances let her in here. We don't want any interference once Blandly's lawyer shows up."

"Yes, sir."

Doug opened the locked door separating the inner offices from the reception area. He stepped out and was immediately confronted by a distraught woman in her early forties. A fashionable and no doubt expensive lilac suit covered a plump body. The jacket was buttoned wrong, and her blond hair needed brushing. It was obvious she'd put her make-up on hastily.

"Excuse me, ma'am. I'm Detective Milligan. Perhaps I can help you." He spoke in a soothing voice.

"I don't think you people realize who I am."

"No, ma'am, perhaps I don't."

She swelled her bosom and patted her hair, though her effort did little to smooth the erratic strands. "I'm Mrs. Clarice Blandly, Councilman Blandly's wife. I'm also the president of the Rocky Bluff Improvement Committee, as well as a prominent member of several other organizations including the Country Club."

"Yes, ma'am."

"I heard that you've arrested my husband on some trumped up charge or other."

"It's true, we have detained your husband."

"What on earth for? You cops are just angry with him because he voted down your pay raise."

"No ma'am."

"Then what is it? Why are you holding him? I have the right to know."

Doug sighed. He knew unless he told her, she'd keep after him until he did. "He allegedly exposed himself to a police officer."

"What are you saying? That's outrageous. Why would he expose himself to a policeman? That doesn't even make sense. My husband is not gay." She stomped her foot and crossed her arms.

"A female police officer, ma'am."

She was quiet for a moment. "You tricked him, didn't you? What are the charges?"

"He's been arrested for lewd behavior."

She huffed and puffed and scowled. "Trumped up charges. There has to be a mistake."

"Ma'am, we have reason to believe he's done this several times in the past few weeks. Today he was caught in the act."

She blinked her eyes a few times. Doug's words seemed to pierce through her emotional armor. Her belligerence disappeared, leaving her deflated. Moaning, she sank onto one of the benches. "Winston promised me he'd never do that again."

Surprised, Doug said, "I think you should wait until your husband's lawyer arrives before you say anything more."

Back on her feet, she pointed to the door. "No, I'm not waiting. He's pushed me too far this time. I'm tired of all of his lies and the vows he never intended to keep. Let me inside and I'll tell you all about my upstanding husband and his unsavory past."

Doug motioned to the receptionist to unlock the door.

■

CHAPTER 11

ABEL DIDN'T HEAR about Councilman Blandly's arrest until the early afternoon when a special report came over the Santa Barbara television channel. A popular female reporter appeared on the screen, standing outside the Rocky Bluff P.D. along with a few others news people with cameras.

Speaking into her handheld microphone she introduced herself and said, "We're in the small town of Rocky Bluff in Ventura County. A prominent businessman and elected official of the Rocky Bluff City Council was arrested today for lewd behavior. Ryan Strickland, Public Relations Officer of the RBPD is here to give an update on the situation."

The camera closed in on Ryan who was his usual composed self. "The investigation of this case has just begun so I can only give you a few facts. Councilman Winston Blandly has been arrested for allegedly exposing himself to women jogging along the beach."

Reporters began shouting out questions.

"What kind of evidence do you have against the councilman?"

"How many women did he expose himself to?"

"Does the councilman have a past history of this kind of activity?"

Ryan smiled and raised a hand for silence. "All I can tell you is we have several eye witness accounts, including a female police officer."

That response caused another flurry of questions.

The Santa Barbara reporter stuck her microphone in front of Ryan's mouth. "What exactly did the councilman do?"

"Several witnesses gave a physical description that matched that of

Councilman Blandly. They said he approached them wearing nothing but an overcoat."

Ryan pointed to a young man waving his hand exuberantly, one Abel recognized as a reporter from the *Rocky Bluff Banner*.

"What will happen to the councilman?"

"I can't predict the outcome, but he has been taken to the Ventura County jail where he'll be arraigned. He'll likely post bail and return home to await trial."

Ryan politely answered a few more questions, but didn't impart any new information. Abel switched off the TV. Interesting, who'd have thought the pervert exposing himself to the women running on the beach would turn out to be one of Rocky Bluff's most influential citizens. Of course, the police officer he'd exposed himself to had to be Stacey.

There was something else he vaguely remembered about a crime on a beach. What was that about? Something important but he just couldn't seem to drag it out of his memory.

Before he could sort out his memories, Lupita called him from the kitchen. "Daddy, can I have some more milk?"

As he headed for the kitchen, the telephone rang. When he answered, his father said, "Your mother seems to be doing a bit better."

"You're still taking her to the doctor, right?"

"Oh yes. First thing Monday morning."

Abel hung up and felt relieved his father planned to follow through with the appointment. Without medical intervention, hope for his mother's mental health was bleak.

"Daddy." Lupita called out again.

Abel opened the refrigerator and took out the milk carton. He wished he could remember what was bothering him about the beach crime—or that he would forget about it all together.

■

The remainder of the day was filled with the usual incidents.

A traffic accident occurred at a busy intersection on the bluff. The residents of the neighborhood had asked the Rocky Bluff City Council to install a stop sign on both streets, to no avail. The council didn't want to spend the money and the stop sign probably wouldn't become a reality until someone was killed.

Elderly neighbors got into a yelling match that escalated into a fist-fight because one had trimmed the limbs growing into his yard from a tree belonging to the other. Officer Aragon responded to the call. The threat of arrest calmed both men down and they re-directed their anger toward Aragon. After another threat of arrest, they regained their good sense. By the time Aragon left, the men worked together to load the cut branches into a trailer to be hauled to the dump.

Another officer on the day shift responded to a call at one of the elementary schools. A teacher thought her purse had been stolen. It turned out, she'd merely misplaced it. She found it before the report could be filed. The same officer's only other call was to check out vandalism of a citizen's car in the parking lot of a fast-food restaurant.

A lost dog and a cat stranded in a tree occupied most of Officer Gordon Butler's afternoon. His last call of the day was a shop-lifting incident. The shop-lifter was a ten-year-old boy who'd been caught on camera hiding a DVD inside his jacket. The furious mother came and asked Butler to take her son to juvenile hall.

He didn't. Instead he lectured the boy. "You don't want to go to juvenile hall. It's not a nice place. The bigger kids will beat you up and they'll take away your food." After Butler pointed out more horrible probabilities of even spending one night in the juvenile facility, the boy's eyes filled with tears.

"I'm sorry, I promise I won't ever steal nothing again." He started to cry. "Please, Mom, don't let him take me away."

The tears did it and the mother hugged her son.

Not as easily moved, Butler retained his stern expression toward the boy. "You're free to take your son home, ma'am, but, young man, if I ever hear learn that you've been shoplifting again, I'll haul you off so fast your head will spin."

The boy's lower lip trembled. "You won't, sir. I promise."

■

The day shift ended and the evening shift began.

The news of Councilman Blandly's arrest had taken over the front page of the *Banner*, relegating stories about the angel in the window to the second page. A large crowd still gathered in front of the furniture store. Officer Vaughn Aragon once again volunteered for a second shift and found himself standing around watching the subdued throng jockeying for spots closer to the angel.

"Do you think it's fading any?" Aragon asked between bites of a huge taco he'd bought at the Mexican catering truck. If nothing else, he'd had some great food because of the strange apparition.

"The angel? Naw, looks the same to me." Felix Zachary stood a head taller than Aragon, but he didn't appear at all formidable in his uniform. People seemed to like Zachary and came up and chatted with him from time-to-time.

"We're getting to be as much of a fixture as the angel." Aragon finished the taco and licked sauce from his fingers. "Hope everything keeps as calm as it has been so far."

"You ought to take a night off," Felix Zachary said. "Aren't you getting tired of working double shifts?"

"Naw. I like it. Don't have nothing better to do."

"Get out and meet people. Make some friends. Don't you have a hobby or something?"

Aragon tilted his head. "Used to enjoy working on my house. Don't have one anymore. Can't even find a drinking buddy."

"That's probably not a bad thing. You interested in dating?"

"Wouldn't be opposed to it."

"I'll talk to my wife, see if she knows any single teachers."

Zachary was right, Vaughn did need to meet people. He sure couldn't go on like this, working double shifts and going home to a TV and beer in that sleazy motel room. What a crappy life. Looking back though, most of his existence had been like that—killing the kid and his divorce weren't the only difficult things he'd survived.

His mother had deserted him and his sister, Muriel, when they were seven and eight. A career Army man, his father couldn't take care of them on his own so he'd shipped them off to his parents. Grandpa Aragon's forefathers had come to this country from Spain. Proud of his heritage, he'd displayed the family crest in the living room. In fact, Grandpa's ancestry was the only thing that made him proud.

He certainly wasn't proud of Vaughn's father, his only son, whom he ridiculed to his grandchildren by calling him a stupid foot soldier who married a tramp. It didn't matter to his grandfather that Sergeant Aragon made sergeant when he was in his early twenties and served valiantly in the Gulf War. Nor did his grandfather care that his son was posthumously awarded the Silver Star after he was killed by enemy fire. More than once, his grandpa said, "Stupid GI didn't have enough sense to stay out of the way."

Even after his son died, Grandpa had nothing good to say about him. Vaughn's grandmother had been loving and sweet to both children and told them stories about their father's childhood. Her son's death had taken a toll on her mental and physical health. It wasn't long after the funeral that she was diagnosed with terminal cancer.

When she died, Vaughn was sixteen and his sister, Muriel, seventeen. Though it didn't seem possible, Grandpa got meaner. He struck out at both of them, verbally and physically, over trivial things like Vaughn forgetting to take out the trash, or Muriel not having dinner on the table when he thought it ought to be. He constantly called Muriel a tramp and predicted she'd turn out like her mother. His favorite tag for Vaughn was a "brain-dead good for nothing."

When she turned eighteen, Muriel got a job as a waitress and found a small apartment to rent. His big sister became Vaughn's salvation when he went to live with her. While finishing high school, he bussed tables at the same place where she worked. He never went back to see his grandfather.

Local cops ate at the diner regularly. One of them noticed Vaughn and encouraged him to enroll in the police science classes at the community college. Since he didn't have any other plans for his future, that's what he did. He managed to get good grades, graduate with an AA degree in Police Science, was accepted in the Academy and when he finished, applied and went to work for LAPD. Not long after that, he met his future wife, fell in love, married and thought his life had finally changed for the better. He was wrong.

Zachary continued on. "I've got an even better idea. You know who's really a good match maker? Ryan's wife, Barbara."

"Oh, yeah?"

"Yeah. I bet if she knew you were looking for some female companionship she'd be tickled to hook you up with somebody. Between Barbara and my wife, they're sure to find someone you might like."

■

Despite being a Friday night, the town was pretty quiet. Abel thought it had something to do with the angel in the window. He decided to go there and check it out. He found Officers Zachary and Aragon leaning against one of the police cars. He double-parked his own unit beside it and got out.

"How're things going?" he asked.

Both officers stood straighter as they greeted Abel, after all he was the duty sergeant. Zachary spoke, "Much like it has every evening. Crowd is behaving. All they're interested in is seeing the angel. What can we do for you, Sergeant?"

Abel was always a bit taken aback when Zachary called him sergeant. They'd both been up for promotion at the same time. Zachary had been the favored candidate until he'd shot and killed the unarmed suspect.

"Not a thing. Nothing's going on so I thought I'd take a look at this angel everyone is so excited about." Abel glanced toward the majority of the congregated people. "That's it over there?"

"Yep. Not too easy to get close, but if you let 'em know you're a cop, and they see your uniform, they'll move out of the way," Aragon said.

Abel walked around the outskirts of the gathering people. He could hear them murmuring among themselves. An old woman supporting herself with a walker glanced at him. "It's a true blessing from God."

Abel nodded and smiled.

Her companion, a younger man, countered with, "I think it's a warning. It's the Lord telling us the end is near and we darn well better change our ways."

Abel was short, and it was impossible for him to see what was captivating everyone's attention. He cleared his throat and took Aragon's advice. "Excuse me. Police officer. Coming through."

Some people glanced at him and reluctantly moved enough to create a narrow path for him. As he made his way through it, he couldn't help brushing against elbows and hips. He got one or two dirty looks, but most folks moved over without looking away from the window of the furniture store.

When he got close enough to see what had been mesmerizing people for the last few evenings, he was shocked. No wonder so many came and returned again and again. He could hardly believe his eyes. A three-dimensional figure seemed to glow right through the plate glass. It almost covered the window. There was no doubt about what the form represented, with the handsome but peaceful face and the huge wings which seemed to ripple as if being blown by a soft breeze. There was no color to it, just a disconcerting brightness. It was an angel.

"My God," Abel breathed.

The person standing nearest him said, "Yes, my God indeed."

Mesmerized, Abel studied it. It didn't look like a reflection, nor was it like a Disney holographic image. It looked like the real thing. He wondered if anyone had gone into the furniture store in the daytime to take a look around. Maybe the image was being projected from the inside. If so, why? What would be the point?

The more he stared at the angel, the more he noticed. The face wasn't like any face he'd ever seen before but had the qualities of many faces. Though not of any easily discernible ethnicity, the features hinted at a variety of nationalities.

Abel focused on the angel's eyes. Unusual, piercing, peaceful, knowing were words that came to mind. It seemed as though the heavenly being looked directly at him, straight into his soul.

Without thinking, he said, "Maria's got to take time off to see this."

Abel jumped when the man who'd spoken previously said, "Yes, she should. Everyone should take the time to see this angel."

The stranger's words broke the spell Abel had fallen under. He returned to Aragon and Zachary, his mind full of wonder—and questions.

■

CHAPTER 12

"AREN'T YOU TAKING the kids to see the angel tonight?" Ryan asked.

After dinner, with reluctant help from the boys, Barbara finished cleaning the kitchen. Instead of urging them to hurry with their homework so the four of them could traipse downtown and see the angel one more time, she sat on the couch next to Ryan.

"I think I've been enough times already and besides, I know I've been neglecting you." She ran the back of her hand down Ryan's cheek.

He caught her hand in his and squeezed. "Marrying you was the best decision I ever made."

"I feel the same way." Her smile was downright flirtatious. "Tell me about your day, sweetheart."

"You heard about the arrest of the man who exposed himself to female joggers at the beach, didn't you?"

"Of course, silly. The officers' wives spread the news way before you made your TV announcement." She cuddled even closer to him. "By the way, you're getting so good at these TV spots I wouldn't be a bit surprised if one of the network news programs didn't offer you a job. You're much better looking than any of their newscasters."

"And you're a bit prejudiced." Ryan laughed but couldn't help wondering if she was buttering him up for some reason.

"Were you as surprised as we were that Councilman Blandly is the guilty party?" Barbara scooted closer to him.

"I think everyone was surprised. He always came across as such a narrow-minded twit. He never listened to an opinion that didn't agree with his. Never had anything good to say about the police department either."

She giggled. "That's because he was always afraid if the city hired more police officers they'd have the time to catch him when he was running around in nothing but an overcoat." Barbara squeezed his knee. "Poor Stacey. That must've been a sight to behold."

Without him giving her any of the details, it sounded like Barbara had already heard everything about the arrest—a perfect example of the wives' network.

"She said the sight of his naked body was so disgusting she didn't recognize him until they brought him into the station and she had time to think about him."

"Yes, all the wives have been giggling over the thought of him. The pompous man would be even more humiliated if he knew he was the subject of our gossip."

Amazing, the women seemed to have ferreted out all the juicy details. "With the arrest and everyone knowing about his perverted behavior, I doubt if he's worried about what the police officer's wives are saying about him."

Barbara snuggled closer. "What's going to happen to him?"

"He'll spend the weekend in county lock-up. Once he's seen a judge, he'll probably get out on bail. What will happen after that is anyone's guess, but I suspect, along with his prior record, his days as a councilman are numbered."

"With him gone, maybe the council will consider pay raises for the department."

"Would be nice." He thought a moment before adding, "Though I have no reason to think any of the rest of others are perverts, none of the council members seem to want to approve anything that costs any money unless it results in new revenues for the city treasury."

She squeezed his hand. "This is nice, isn't it? We haven't sat down and had a conversation between just the two of us in a long while. Seems like we're always dashing here and there. If it isn't something for the kids it's..." Her voice trailed off.

"The unlikely appearance of an angel."

"Well, yes, though that wasn't what I was going to say." She gazed at him with those big eyes of hers.

Here it came, whatever it was she'd been planning on ever since she sat down beside him. "And what was that?"

"Don't forget tomorrow is the big day."

Big day? What was she talking about? Oh, of course. "The wedding. Stacey's and Doug's."

"Yes, and I have a favor to ask you."

He knew it was something. "Sure, honey, whatever I can manage."

"I promised Stacey I'd come early and help her get into her gown at the church. Could you see that the boys get into their good clothes and bring them to the church when it's closer to the time for the wedding?"

That was all? "Sure, no problem." He felt a tad embarrassed because he'd expected something far more complicated.

"Great. Don't worry. I'll have their clothes set out for them. It'll only be a matter of making sure they get ready on time."

"I think I can handle that." At times, Barbara made him feel like an incompetent jerk. Of course, he'd had no prior experience being a father, but he and the boys managed to get along okay. She acted like he couldn't manage the simplest of tasks that related to her sons.

"I know you can." She reached over, gently moved his head towards hers and kissed him.

Any suspicion he'd felt earlier disappeared.

■

Rocky Bluff had been quiet, quieter than most Friday evenings. Abel attributed it to the fact that so many citizens were hanging around the furniture store on Valley Boulevard contemplating the angel. The police part of his brain felt sure the phenomena was a trick of some sort—though he couldn't fathom any reason for anyone to do that, since no one was making a profit except possibly the taco truck parked down the block. The religious part of his brain couldn't help wondering if it really was a sign from God.

Zachary called in to let him know that the crowd had grown even larger, the biggest it had been since the angel had first been noticed. Everyone continued to behave, probably because of the spiritual association of the vision.

On his break, he called Maria. "I saw the angel tonight."

She paused before speaking. "Angel? Oh, the angel in the window of the furniture store. Some of the nurses at work were talking about that. What does it look like?"

"It's quite amazing. I've never seen anything like it. The angel is shiny, iridescent-like. It's so bright, it almost hurt my eyes to look at."

"What's causing it?"

"I haven't the faintest idea. Once I'd looked at it for a minute or two a kind of calming effect came over me, a peaceful feeling. That's probably why there've been no problems with the crowds congregating around."

"So you think it's really a God thing?" She sounded skeptical.

"I don't know what to think. I'm glad I got to see it though."

"If you're happy, I'm happy. Listen, Abel, I called your dad and told him how important it was that he get your mom to that doctor's appointment. He assured me he would. He's also glad everyone understands about her problem now."

"That's good." Abel still didn't feel comfortable talking about his mother and what was happening to her. "How's Lupita doing?"

"Great. She always wants me to read the same story to her at bedtime, but she finishes almost every sentence before I can."

"She does that with me too."

"Oh, and don't forget about tomorrow."

"What's tomorrow?"

"Abel, you know. Doug and Stacey's wedding."

He chuckled. "I was kidding. The wedding is the main subject of conversation at the station. Nearly everyone is going. We'll only have a skeleton crew tomorrow."

■

Doug could hardly contain himself. He'd checked his suit to make sure it was still pressed and brushed off imaginary lint. He polished his dress shoes, even though they didn't need it. He raced up and down the stairs several times without remembering why.

"For Pete's sake, Doug, settle down, you're making me nervous." Gordon hollered from his favorite spot on the couch, TV tuned to a baseball game.

"I can't relax." Doug ran his fingers through his freshly cut hair. "I've been so anxious for tomorrow to come and now it's almost here. I'm so jittery I wonder if I'll make it through the ceremony."

"You will, don't worry."

"Don't let me forget that I promised to stop at the florist and pick up Stacey's bouquet or nosegay or whatever it's called."

"I'll remind you as soon as we're ready to leave."

"What about the ring? Did I give it to you already? I can't remember where I put it."

Gordon guffawed. "I've never seen you so rattled. You gave me the ring, don't you remember? I have it in the pocket of my suit. My suit is hanging on the back of the door of my room. Why don't you have a beer? Sit down and relax."

"A beer sounds good. I'll sit, but I don't think I can relax." He grabbed a beer out of the refrigerator and plopped down on the other end of the couch. His knee kept jumping up and down. He tried to keep it still with no success.

■

Stacey had gone to bed early to get a good night's rest so she'd be her best for the wedding, but no matter how she tried she couldn't sleep. Her excitement about her wedding kept her tossing and turning. At midnight she squinted at her bedside clock. Was it too late to call Doug? Maybe he was having the same problem.

She reached over and scooped her cell phone from the nightstand and dialed Doug's number. The first ring hadn't completed when Doug answered, "Stacey? Is something wrong?"

"I can't sleep."

He laughed. "I haven't even gone to bed yet. I keep thinking there's something more I need to do."

"I can't calm down enough to fall asleep. We'll be a great pair tomorrow with bags under our eyes."

"Honey, you'll be a beautiful bride no matter what. I love you, Stacey. I can't wait to hear the minister say we're husband and wife."

She yawned. "Maybe I just needed to hear your voice. I actually feel like I might be able to sleep."

"Here's to sweet dreams for both of us."

"See you tomorrow." She giggled. "Don't forget, it's bad luck for the groom to see the bride before the ceremony."

"You don't believe in that old superstition, do you?"

"Not really. After all, we're not having a big wedding, so none of that traditional stuff counts."

"I love you so much, I don't care about any of the ceremonial part. All I want is for us to be husband and wife."

"Me too." She yawned again. "I really do think I can fall asleep now. Love you."

"Love you too, Stacey. Goodnight."

■

Vaughn Aragon stretched out on the narrow mattress of the cheap motel room he called home. Maybe if he could find a better place to live he wouldn't feel so depressed. He'd studied his surroundings so often even with his eyes closed he could remember all the scruffy details. He noted the wallpaper peeling in the corner, the dark stain on the ceiling tile from the leaking roof, the threadbare places on the muddy brown carpet, the cigarette burns on the pine dresser, the chips in the ceramic sink, and the ugly stains in the toilet bowl.

Worst of all was the moldy stench that permeated everything, and even clung to his uniform. Opening the windows didn't help much, though sometimes the scent of the ocean drifted in.

Vaughn now realized being an officer at the Rocky Bluff P.D. was a dead-end job. He'd heard he was lucky to get the transfer in. Not so lucky. Unless someone retired or died, there was no chance for advancement in this dinky department. The pay was far less than what he'd made working for LAPD. Of course, he had to admit it was much cheaper living here, which made up for the decrease in salary. The opportunity to work the extra shift helped too. He volunteered to do it again tomorrow night.

The men he'd met were okay, but no one seemed to have room in their lives for a new buddy. At least in L.A. there were other guys like him whose circumstances had taken a down-turn and liked to get together for a few beers once in awhile. And he could always count on some female around who liked to hang out around cops. He'd made a big mistake, that was for sure, and he didn't see any chance of changing his current situation.

The way things were headed, there wasn't much point in living.

When he finally fell asleep, he once again dreamt about the kid he shot.

The boy got up from the floor, blood pouring from bullet holes. He pointed his gun at Vaughn and started shooting.

Vaughn woke in a sweat. He bolted upright because, for a moment, he thought he saw the kid standing at the foot of his bed. He rubbed his eyes and looked again. No one was there. He put his head back on the pillow.

He'd been told over and over it was a justified shooting. Why couldn't he accept that and get it out of his mind?

■

Abel straightened his desk and finished all the paperwork for the shift. This was the quietest Friday night he could remember. It seemed everyone in town was behaving. No exciting calls. Not much time left until he could sign out and go home.

Several file folders stacked on his computer tower caught his eye. He ought to go through them and chuck out anything that was no longer needed—or file it somewhere.

He plunked the folders down in front of him. The first one he opened contained several faxes and emails. He sorted through them. When he came to the one that he'd received about the time he'd learned about his mother's Alzheimer's, he realized this was what had been wriggling around in his brain and he couldn't remember.

He stared at the faxed bulletin, reading it more carefully than he had the first time. Over the last nine months, young women had disappeared in the state of Washington and down through Oregon. All of the disappearances had happened in small coastal communities. So far, no bodies had turned up. The latest reported disappearance was from the town of Whitethorn on the far northern coast of California. The missing woman was twenty-six. She worked as a waitress and was the mother of a toddler. Not too many more details. It was signed by an FBI agent named Tanner Benedict, followed by a contact phone number and e-mail address.

This was probably information he should pass on to the chief since Rocky Bluff fit the description of a small coastal community.

He made a copy of the fax and dropped it into Chief McKenzie's mail slot on his way out. The chief wouldn't see it until Monday, but Abel didn't think it urgent.

■

CHAPTER 13

STACEY MANAGED TO get a few hours of sleep. When she awoke, her eyes flew open and she smiled. Nervous anticipation morphed into an excitement she could hardly contain. She glanced at her watch. Six a.m. Too much time until her wedding.

Jogging might clear her head. Give her a chance to expend some energy and help sort out her thoughts.

She slipped on a T-shirt, jogging shorts and shoes. When she left her room, she peeked in on Davey. Love surged through her. Fast asleep, he snuggled down, nearly hidden by the covers.

She could hear her mom bustling around in the kitchen, but her father didn't seem to be awake yet. She found Clara dressed in her bathrobe, mixing a bowl of what looked like pancake batter. "Hi, Mom." She kissed her cheek.

Without looking, her mother said, "All ready for your big day?"

"More than ready. I'm so excited I can hardly stand it."

Clara turned, frowning as she surveyed her daughter's clothes. "Why are you dressed like that?"

"I had trouble sleeping last night. I'm going for a quick jog. When I get back, I'll eat breakfast and take a shower."

"Oh, sweetheart, do you think that's a good idea?"

"I felt so good jogging along the beach the last couple of days. Now that we don't have to worry about perverted Councilman Blandly, I'll have a great time."

"Seems to me if it were me going to be married this morning, I'd have better things to do than going off to run." Clara stirred the pancake batter so vigorously some slopped out on her bathrobe.

"Don't worry, I won't be gone long." Once Stacey had tried explaining to her mother about the euphoria that enveloped her when she ran, but her mother couldn't seem to grasp the concept.

"What should I tell Doug if he calls?"

"Exactly what I told you. I'm going jogging on the beach. Don't worry, Mom. I'll be back in less than an hour."

She glanced at her watch and smiled at her diamond engagement ring. Soon it would be joined by a matching wedding band. "I'll be back by seven-thirty at the latest."

■

"Did I hear something about pancakes?" Clyde came into the kitchen already in his suit pants and a white shirt. He kissed his wife's cheek.

"You sure did. I just put them on. There's bacon there in the warming dish." Clara pointed to a ceramic bowl on the table with a tea towel over the top.

Barefoot and in his pajamas, Davey asked, "Where's Mommy?"

"She'll be back in a few minutes, Sweetie, she went out for a run." Clara poured some batter onto the griddle. "Sit down and I'll have some pancakes for you in a jiffy."

"To tell you the truth, the smell of bacon is what lured me here." Clyde lifted the napkin, snagged a couple of pieces and gave them to Davey. He got another piece, held it with his fingers and nibbled on it. "Did I hear you say Stacey went for a run? I thought she'd be bustling around here, having a bubble-bath, prettying herself all up for her groom."

"Yep, she did." Davey licked the bacon grease from his fingers.

"That surprises me. Doesn't seem like the sort of thing a bride would do on her wedding day." It certainly wasn't the way Stacey had acted before her first wedding.

"Mystified me too. Here's your pancakes." Clara put a plate with two pancakes on it in front of Davey, and another in front of her husband. "I wonder if I should go ahead and make the rest of the pancakes—or save some batter and cook Stacey's when she gets back."

"How long has she been gone?" Clyde knew Stacey enjoyed jogging. He supposed she wanted to run off her pre-wedding jitters.

"She left a bit after six, said she'd be back by seven-thirty at the latest."

Clyde glanced at his watch. "It's past that. Why don't you go ahead and finish with the cooking. She ought to be popping in here any minute."

Clara fixed the rest of the pancakes. She sat and ate two herself, but her brow was furrowed and she appeared anxious. "Stacey ought to be back by now."

In an effort to calm his wife, he said, "Don't worry, sweetheart, she probably ran into someone she knew, or maybe she thought of some last minute thing to take care of. Why don't you get ready and I'll help Davey."

"Good idea. I know she wanted to leave for the church before ten. Her plan was to shower here, but finish dressing at the church. That nice Barbara Strickland is going to help her."

Clara stood and didn't even bother to clear off the table, a sure sign her mind was only on her daughter's welfare.

The phone rang at half past eight. Clyde answered, hoping it might be Stacey.

It was Doug calling for Stacey. "I know it's a bit early, but Stacey called me late last night and I wanted to make sure she was up."

"She left to go jogging around six," Clyde said. "We're beginning to worry. We expected her back awhile ago."

"Where was she going to run? Around the park?"

"No, Clara said she was going to the beach."

After a slight pause, Doug said, "I better go look for her."

"I'd like to say that you probably don't need to, but I have to confess I'm a bit concerned. She really should be back by now."

"I'll head down there now. Maybe she's having car trouble."

"Thanks, Doug. Will you please give me a call as soon as you find her?"

"Sure thing."

Clara came out of the bedroom dressed for the wedding wearing a turquoise dress with a lace tunic jacket Stacey that had picked out for her. "Who was on the phone?"

"Doug. He's going to look for Stacey."

"Why don't we give her a call on her cell phone. She always has it with her." Clara picked up the kitchen phone and pressed the numbers for her daughter's cell phone. It rang and rang, then the automatic voice came on asking the calling party to leave a message. "This is your mother. Please get in touch with us right away." She put the phone back into its holder. "She's not answering. I don't like this."

"Let's not get all upset." He attempted to sound calm, but his stomach felt like a big ball of hot lead.

"I can't imagine anything more important to Stacey than coming home to get ready for her wedding." Clara's eyes filled with tears.

"Doug will be calling any minute to let us know he found her." Clyde hoped his prediction was true, but he felt a crawling sensation on the back of his neck.

Davey came down the hall. "Grandpa, you said you were gonna help me with my clothes."

"I'm ready. I'll do it." Clara went to Davey and turned him around but not before giving Clyde a pleading look.

■

"What's going on?" Gordon asked.

Breakfast was on the table, but Doug made the phone call to Stacey's house before he sat down to eat.

Doug wore his good suit, along with the shirt and tie. Still barefoot, he slid his feet into an old pair of sneakers he kept by the back door. He grabbed his car keys and headed toward the front of the house.

Gordon raised out of his chair. "Has something happened? Anything I can do?"

Doug ignored the questions. "I'll be back as soon as I can."

He jumped into his SUV, started it, backed out of the driveway and headed toward the beach. He didn't even want to consider the possibilities. As a police officer he'd worked on several missing persons' cases. Sometimes people disappeared because they wanted to. Usually it was because something overwhelming was happening in their lives, and it was easier to walk away than face whatever was going on. Surely this wasn't what happened with Stacey, she'd been excited about the wedding.

Besides, when she'd called last night, she'd given no indication of anything being wrong, or that she had any second thoughts about getting married. No, that couldn't be it.

The scenario he'd given her father had to be the answer. Something was wrong with her car. But why hadn't she called either one of them? Maybe her cell phone needed recharging.

There were other, more frightening possibilities. Perhaps she'd had an accident, either in her car or when she was running on the beach. He quickly dialed the police station.

"This is Detective Milligan. Have there been any accident reports this morning?"

The answer was "no." All was quiet.

In a missing person's case, and the person in question is a competent adult, the police department usually didn't take action for twenty-four hours. This would not be the situation with Stacey.

In his mind, Doug went over the points that he told someone who suspected a loved one was missing. First, check the home, make sure the loved one wasn't hiding, fallen or hurt. He remembered one more thing. He quickly dialed Stacey's home. Clyde answered.

When Doug identified himself, Clyde jumped in with, "Did you find her? Is she all right?"

"No, sir, I haven't reached the beach yet. I want you to do something for me."

"Of course."

"Check her room. Make sure she didn't leave a note. See if anything is out of order. If you find anything, anything at all, call me right back on this number."

Clyde assured him he and Clara would do as asked, but doubted there would be anything.

"I know, but just in case."

Doug's next call was to the dispatcher again. "I need Officer Aragon's cell number."

He was nearing the beach when he reached Aragon. "Detective Milligan here. I need some information from you. Where did Officer Wilbur leave her car when you and she were after Councilman Blandly?"

"What's going on?" Aragon asked.

Doug had a hard time saying it. "Stacey's missing. She left home early this morning to go for a jog on the beach. No one has seen or heard from her since."

"She parked on Seagull. I'll be right there and help you look for her."

"Thanks, man." Having Aragon helping meant they could cover more ground in a shorter period of time.

The yellow VW was parked right where Aragon had said. Doug didn't know whether to feel relieved or not. He approached the car cautiously, but no sign of Stacey. Both doors were locked.

The next thing on the check list when someone was missing was to contact family, friends and the person's work place to see if anyone knew anything or had seen the person. Because Doug knew exactly where Stacey had been and she'd gone to the place she'd told her folks she was going, that step wasn't necessary. His hope and prayer was that once he walked out onto the beach, he'd see Stacey jogging toward him.

A siren howled in the distance. In minutes a police car raced into the parking lot and screeched to a halt. Wearing his uniform, the stocky Aragon climbed out. "She's not here?"

"No. There's no sign of a struggle. She's got to still be on the beach somewhere. How far did she jog?"

"Usually as far as the fancy restaurant and then she turned around and came back. Let's find her."

Together, the men headed over the sand dune and down toward the ocean. Though it was a gray day and a dark fog bank hung off shore, the visibility was good. Three children darted back and forth, squealing as foamy waves splashed against their bare feet and legs. A woman, probably their mother, sat farther away on the sand reading a book.

As far as Doug could see, the rest of the beach was deserted. "I'll talk to that woman, ask if she saw Stacey or anyone else out here."

"I'll go down the beach, see if I can spot her or anything suspicious." Aragon took off, stepping slowly and deliberately. He looked like he knew what he was doing.

Doug approached the woman. Obviously startled, she gasped. He pulled out his identification. "Detective Milligan. I'm looking for any information about a female jogger you might have seen this morning. She is five-five, short, light hair."

The woman pulled off her dark glasses and squinted at his credentials before answering. "Sorry, Detective. The kids and I arrived about fifteen minutes ago and I haven't seen anyone. We were the first ones out here."

Doug thanked her. His heart pounded so hard his ears hurt. "What about in the parking lot? Did you see anyone there? Or when you were driving toward the beach? Anything that might be helpful?"

She shrugged. "With three kids in the car I'm lucky to see where I'm going."

He pulled one of his cards from his wallet and handed it to her. "If you think of something, anything, give me a call. Please, this is very important."

Oh God. Where could Stacey be? What happened to her? Doug headed off as the kids came running to their mother, probably to find out what he was asking her about.

A pair of seagulls screeched in the sky above him, echoing the screaming in his brain—Stacey, where are you?

He trudged through the sand. It sifted into his shoes, making walking uncomfortable, but he had only one thought on his mind. Find Stacey.

He suspected she probably ran in the damp sand. Any footprints she might have left, the ocean quickly erased.

Up ahead, Aragon stopped. Had he found something?

■

CHAPTER 14

CLARA AND CLYDE stood in Stacey's room, staring. The bed wasn't made, not surprising. Under a clear plastic cover, their daughter's pale blue wedding dress hung on the back of the door. On her dresser sat an open make-up case. Folded neatly inside were two pairs of panty hose, a wisp of a slip, along with blush, eye-makeup, and a hairbrush.

"All things she planned to take over to the church," Clara said. Shoes that matched the dress sat on the floor.

"Do you see anything out of place?" Clyde asked.

Clara fought back tears. "No. You can tell Doug there's nothing. No notes, no indication that she planned to do anything but jog and come straight home to shower and get ready for her wedding."

Something caught Clara's attention. "Oh no."

"What?"

"Look." Clara pointed to the nightstand. "Her cell phone. She left it here."

"No wonder she hasn't called." Clyde folded Clara into his arms. "It's time we took some action too."

"What can we do?"

"The most important thing, pray."

"Oh, sweetheart, I've been doing that ever since we realized something was wrong."

"I think we should get in touch with Barbara Strickland. Maybe she's heard something. We can let her know what's happened."

"But we don't know that anything's happened. We just don't know where Stacey is at the moment." Clara's voice rose and she felt panic overtaking her.

Clyde hugged her tighter. "Call Barbara. It's better to do something."

"Don't let Davey know anything is wrong. I don't want him to worry."

"I think we have to tell Davey, there's no way to keep it from him. Things may get hectic before it's all over. People will start arriving at the church in little over an hour. We're going to have to be there to greet them."

"Surely Stacey will turn up by then. She's been so looking forward to this day. I can't think of anything that would keep her from missing her wedding."

Clyde nodded and took his arms from around his wife. "Honey, call Barbara."

It was all she could do to keep from sobbing. Only the fact that she didn't want Davey to know how upset she was kept her from giving in to her emotions.

"I'll talk to Davey and get him ready. You call Barbara. I'll use my cell to call Doug to let him know we didn't find anything. When we're finished, I think we should go to the church."

Clara dialed Barbara's number and she answered on the first ring, sounding out of breath. "Hello."

"Barbara, this is Clara Osborne, Stacey's mother."

"Oh, hi, Mrs. Osborne. I was just heading out the door to go to the church."

"We've got a big problem." Clara could hardly speak.

"You sound upset. What's the matter? Can I help?"

The emotion she'd contained inside spilled out through her words. "Stacey is missing." Clara swallowed hard before continuing. "She went jogging and never came back. We don't know what's happened to her."

Dead silence was followed by a somber sounding Barbara. "Does Doug know?"

"Yes, he's out looking for her now, but we haven't heard from him for awhile. Have you? Did Stacey call you this morning?"

"No, I'm sorry. I haven't heard from either of them. What do you want me to do?"

"My husband and I are going to the church in a few minutes."

"All right. I'll let my husband know what's going on, and then I'll go to the church too. And, Mrs. Osborne, I'll be praying for her safety."

"Thank you." No longer able to pretend any longer, Clara hung up the phone and allowed the tears to flow.

■

Barbara said a quick prayer for Stacey while heading down the hallway to the bedroom where Ryan was dressing for the wedding. He sat on the bed, leaning over to put on his shoes.

"Ryan."

He peered at her, surprise in his expression. "I thought you were leaving. Who was on the phone?"

"Stacey's mother. She said Stacey went jogging this morning and never returned. Doug's out looking for her now."

Ryan jammed his feet into his shoes and stood. "Where did she go jogging?"

"I didn't ask. Mrs. Osborne wants me to go to the church. I'll take the boys with me. I know you'll want to help."

"I'll call Doug, find out what's going on and what he wants me to do. I wonder if he's made a formal report yet."

"I don't know anymore than what I've told you."

"Okay. You go ahead." He took his cell phone from his dresser, flipped it open and started his call.

Barbara hurried to the boys' rooms. "Come on guys, we've got to go now."

A bevy of groans and complaints including, "I'm not ready," greeted her.

"Doesn't matter. You'll have to go like you are." If through God's grace, the wedding came off on time, Barbara figured Stacey and the guests would have to excuse her sons' appearance.

She herded them out to the family's van. Surprisingly, Tony, the eldest was in his dress pants and shirt, though he still wore his favorite Nikes on his feet and his hair stood in tufts. Daryl had his good shirt on, but it hung over his faded blue jeans and, of course, he hadn't changed out of his worn sneakers. The youngest, Philip, had managed to put on his Sunday trousers and shoes, but he still had on his pajama top. She grabbed his good shirt off the door knob as they left the room. None of the boys had combed their hair—but that could be easily remedied when there was time.

Once everyone was settled in the van, Tony, who sat in the front with Barbara, lowered his voice and asked, "What's wrong, Mom? You're acting like something bad happened."

Barbara started the car and backed out of the driveway. "Stacey Wilbur is missing. She went jogging this morning and didn't come back. Doug Milligan is looking for her."

"Maybe she changed her mind and decided she didn't want to get married. Happens all the time on TV and in the movies."

"Stacey and Doug love each other. She could hardly wait to get married. Something or someone is preventing her from coming home." Now that she'd put her worry into words, Barbara prayed that her husband could put something into motion that would hasten Stacey's recovery. She knew Stacey was either hurt or something worse had happened to her.

"Someone would have to be pretty dumb to grab a policewoman," Tony said.

From the back seat, Daryl piped up. "Someone grabbed Officer Wilbur?"

Philip joined in. "Let's go find her."

"Detective Milligan is looking for her, and by this time, I imagine Ryan has got others out searching for her too. I want you boys to pray Officer Wilbur will come home safely and soon."

Barbara glanced in the rearview mirror long enough to see her sons' expressions. She could tell they'd much rather be part of the action than praying. "Prayers are important. God can do what people can't."

"Stacey's kind of little. She probably couldn't fight back." Philip crossed himself and Barbara knew he was praying.

■

The first thing Ryan did was call Doug's cell.

Doug answered. He sounded frantic.

"Ryan here, have you found anything?"

"Maybe a place where there might have been a struggle. It's hard to tell in the sand."

"Is there anyone there with you?"

"The new guy, Aragon. He knew where Stacey parked her car. It's still there."

"What do you want me to do?"

"I'm not sure. There's so little to go on." It was obvious Doug was having a difficult time coming up with any ideas.

"Why don't we get a dog handler? Maybe a dog could follow her scent." Rocky Bluff P.D. didn't have any police dogs—that was one of the department's requests that had been turned down several times by the city council.

"Okay. And could you let the chief know?"

"I'll get right on it. He'll probably authorize a public announcement. Keep looking around down there, but try not to track through that place where you think there might have been a struggle."

Ryan called Chief McKenzie at home and gave him what he knew about Stacey's disappearance. The chief was horrified by the news. Ryan told him what he wanted to do and was given permission.

Before hanging up, the chief added, "Call the dispatcher. Get everyone who is available out on the street. I'll call Ventura P.D. to request a K-9 handler and dog who specializes in tracking ASAP."

Ryan's next call was to the dispatcher. She was told to alert all the on-duty officers as well as those who were off. "As per Chief McKenzie's order, this is to be handled as a high-priority situation."

Next on his list was the local TV and radio stations. He gave both of them Stacey's description, where she was last seen, and numbers to call for anyone with information. Instead of having a TV newscaster come to the police department, Ryan offered to come into the television station to tape an announcement.

■

When the call came through, Abel and Maria were getting dressed for the wedding. Immediately, his mind went to the fax he'd forgotten and finally put in the chief's mailbox. "Oh, God, please, no," he groaned, hoping Stacey's disappearance wasn't related.

Maria poked her head out of the bedroom. "What was that? Are you being called in? Don't people know Stacey and Doug are getting married today?"

"Stacey's missing."

"What?"

"No one knows where she is."

Maria's mouth dropped open. When she caught her breath, she said, "Oh, my God. Poor Doug, poor Stacey."

Lupita poked her head around her mother and hugged her legs.

"I've got to call the chief. I may know something."

"How could you know anything? You've been here with me since you got off work and this morning."

"I don't have time to explain."

"What do you want me to do?" Maria asked.

"Take Lupita to the church. That's where everyone will be. Hopefully it's nothing and Stacey will arrive any minute."

"I can tell by your face, you don't believe what you just said." Tears slid down Maria's cheeks. "Oh, Abel."

"Mama," Lupita cried.

"Do what you have to do." Maria scooped their daughter into her arms. "Lupita and I will wait for you at the church."

Abel called the chief's home number, but his wife said he'd gone into work. When he called the department, the chief hadn't arrived yet. He rushed outside and found Maria putting Lupita into her car seat. He kissed both of them. "I'm heading to the station."

Driving, the mantra he repeated in his mind was, "Please don't let it be what I'm thinking about that fax."

He ran down the hall toward the chief's office. Without knocking, Abel entered the secretary's office and burst through the inner door. Chief McKenzie was at his desk, glasses perched near the end of his nose, telephone to his ear. He nodded at Abel as he finished his conversation. "That'll be perfect. They should go to Seagull Street. One of our officers will meet you there."

He disconnected but didn't replace the receiver. "Have to make one more call, then I'll get to you." McKenzie dialed another number. "The tracking dog and his trainer will be there in about twenty minutes. I'll send one of the officers to meet them. Have someone bring you a piece of Stacey's clothing—something she wore recently." A pause. "Don't worry, we'll find her." He listened again, and hung up.

"What can I do for you, Sergeant? Is this something about Wilbur's disappearance?"

Abel stood in front of the desk. "I'm not sure. In fact I hope not. Did you look at what was in your mailbox?"

"Not since I came in. What is it?"

"Hang on. I'll be right back." Abel retrieved the fax he'd folded and put into the chief's box and hurried back with it. "This came about three days ago. I filed it and forgot about it."

He handed the paper to Chief McKenzie who scanned it quickly. A frown furrowed his brow. "You don't think....?"

"I don't want to, but maybe we should call the F.B.I. agent whose number is there."

"Oh, Lord." McKenzie sighed, pulled the paper nearer and dialed the number. "Agent Benedict, please."

McKenzie listened and nodded. "This is Chief McKenzie of the Rocky Bluff P.D. We have a situation here that you ought to look into."

He listened again. "Yes. One of our female officers has disappeared."

He answered another question. "She wasn't in uniform. She was jogging on the beach."

Obviously the next question asked was for her description.

"She's small, five foot five. Young. Yes, and sweet looking." He paused and listened for a few moments.

"No, she's not married. She was getting married today, that's why we're sure there's foul play involved."

He listened for a few moments and then said sharply, "No, that's not it. She's marrying one of our detectives. He's found a spot where it looks like there might have been a struggle. We've called for a tracking dog. It'll be here soon."

McKenzie was quiet for a longer time, but he kept nodding even though the person on the other end couldn't see him. Finally, he continued, "Yes, Agent Benedict, I'll be here in my office waiting." He replaced the receiver.

He turned in his chair to face Abel. "He should be here in about an hour. He's been visiting small towns along the coast. He says the M.O. isn't quite right, but Stacey fits some of the characteristics of the missing women cases he's been investigating."

■

Waiting was painful. Doug and Aragon kept watch over the place in the sand where there might have been a struggle. It was nothing more than a depression that could've been made by a dog rolling around. But there was nothing else to go on.

Doug wanted action. He would've been happier to be searching for Stacey, but had no idea where to start.

A few more people had come down to enjoy time along the shore. Two young women in bathing suits spread their towels and lay down to sunbathe. Another mother with three children settled close to the first mother. They acted like they knew each other. A couple strolled close to the waterline. All stared curiously at the uniformed cop and the man in a suit, seemingly doing nothing.

Stacey's father trudged across the sand, wearing a suit and carrying a paper sack. He approached Doug who stopped him before he came too near the spot he and Aragon guarded. Clyde held out the sack. "The shorts and T-shirt Stacey slept in last night. Is that what you wanted?"

Doug nodded and took the sack. "Perfect."

Clyde compressed his lips and swallowed hard. "Be honest with me, Doug, what do you think happened to her?"

"I don't know. We think there might have been a struggle here. We're expecting a tracking dog and his trainer anytime now." Doug struggled to sound optimistic.

Nodding, Clyde said, "I know you'll do everything you can. Just remember, Stacey is a scrapper. There is nothing she wanted more than this wedding."

"I know."

Aragon moved closer to Clyde and stuck out his hand. "Sir, I'm Vaughn Aragon. I've partnered with your daughter a couple of times. Believe me, we'll do everything we can to find her and bring her back for her wedding."

Clyde accepted the handshake. His eyes glistened with tears. "Thank you." He turned abruptly and marched back the way he'd come.

Doug watched his departure and before he reached the sand dune that led to the street where Stacey left her car, a small stocky woman in uniform passed him, straining to hold back a dark German Shepherd on a lead.

CHAPTER 15

THE ZACHARYS WERE on their way to the wedding ceremony when Felix got the call about Stacey's disappearance. He answered, listened, and burst loose with a string of swear words.

Wendy turned to him, her eyes wide. "Felix, what on earth is the matter?" She had never heard Felix swear, though she knew he probably kept himself in check around her.

He shook his head, listened some more before responding. "I'll come in." He closed his phone.

Concerned and puzzled, she asked, "What's going on?" All sorts of ideas had popped in her mind, a national disaster or a huge pile-up on the freeway. Though the national disaster could've caused the bad language, she didn't think a freeway accident would.

He pulled the car over to the curb. "I'm going to have to go back home."

"I gathered as much, but what about the wedding?"

"Doesn't look like there'll be one, at least not today."

"What are you talking about? "

"Stacey's missing."

That was a circumstance Wendy hadn't considered. "Missing? What does that mean?"

"From what little I was told, she went jogging at the beach this morning and didn't come back. The chief has called everyone in. I have to get back home and change into my uniform. Do you want to come back with me or go on to the church? I understand most of the wives have gone there. I can drop you off first if that's what you want."

There was plenty she could do at home, but could she focus while worrying about Stacey's well-being? If she went to the church, she'd be updated on what was going on along with the rest of the wives. "Drop me off at the church."

Felix didn't say a word during the two block drive. When they reached Rocky Bluff Community Church, he leaned across her big belly and opened the door. "Are you sure you'll be okay? What if you need to get home?"

She unhooked her seat belt, leaned over and kissed him. "I'm sure someone will be willing to take me if I do. Call me if you find out anything new." The parking lot held many vehicles, she wouldn't be waiting alone.

The large sanctuary was decorated for the wedding. Blue bows flanked the end of each pew. Two large bouquets of white roses and blue delphiniums decorated the sides of the stage. All the people were gathered in the first few rows. Some standing, others sitting, several hugging one another. Five or six knelt on the first steps leading to the pulpit. Reverend Cookmeyer, his head bowed, stood beside Stacey's parents, all obviously in prayer.

Despite the primary reason for the gathering, the atmosphere was somber. More like a funeral than a wedding. Wendy shuddered at the thought. She made her way down the middle aisle.

Barbara Strickland turned around and motioned to her. She nudged her three boys to scoot over and made a place for Wendy.

Sliding in beside her, Wendy whispered, "Has there been any news?"

In a quiet voice, Barbara said, "The last Ryan told me is that he's taping a public service announcement at the TV station. They plan to air it every half hour."

"Surely that will help."

Barbara squeezed Wendy's hand. "I hope so. How are you feeling, dear?"

"Physically, fine, but this news about Stacey is horrible. I can't get my mind around it."

"Pray for her. That's what we've all been doing. That's about the only thing we can do while we sit here and wait."

■

The dog handler reached Doug and Officer Aragon. Her first words were, "Who are we looking for?"

Doug blinked. The officer wore a dark blue, short-sleeved uniform that displayed muscular biceps, probably from working her dog. She was near the same age and height as Stacey, though carried about fifteen more pounds. Her straight, dark brown hair was cut in a short bob.

Aragon spoke first. "Officer Stacey Wilbur. About your size, light hair, wearing jogging shorts and tank top."

The officer, whose name tag identified her as Calvani, said, "What's the thinking here? Abduction?"

"We don't know." Doug glanced at his watch. "We were supposed to get married in about an hour."

Calvani stared at him. "Any problems between you? Last minute cold feet, maybe?"

Doug fought the anger that flared. "No, nothing like that. Everything was fine last night when we talked on the phone. Her folks said she had everything out and ready to take to the church. Besides, she has a little boy. She'd never leave him."

"You have some personal item of hers for my dog?"

Doug held up the sack containing Stacey's shorts and T-shirt. "Her dad brought these to us. She slept in them last night." He handed the sack to Calvani. When she pulled out the items with her gloved hands, he caught a wisp of Stacey's scent. Tears stung his eyes.

Neither Calvani or Aragon acted like they noticed. She held the clothing under her dog's snout. She gave a command in what sounded like German. The dog sniffed all around the depressed area.

The shepherd's ears pointed straight up as he headed over the sand toward the nearest dune. Hanging tightly onto the leash, Calvani trotted behind her dog. Aragon and Doug followed.

The dog paused, sniffed the ground, glanced back at his trainer and strained against his leash as he climbed the sand dune. At the top, the dog stopped. Calvani let him sniff the clothing again. The dog bolted ahead, Calvani struggling to keep up.

A glimmer of hope tantalized Doug as he clambered up the dune, sand filling his shoes at every stop. When he reached the crest, his hope shattered. He could see the parking area at the end of the street. Nothing was there, no vehicles, no people, nothing.

The dog circled. Sniffed the asphalt. Circled again.

Doug ran down the hill, his feet sinking in the dune to his ankles. "What's wrong? What's that mean?" He could tell by the expression on her face the answer wouldn't be encouraging, and it wasn't.

"The scent's gone. Whoever snatched Officer Wilbur put her in a vehicle and drove off. This is all my dog can do." She knelt down and petted the shepherd, speaking German in a soothing voice. Looking up at Doug, she said, "I'm sorry. Really I am."

"Thank you." Doug felt helpless and hopeless. Now he knew the worst, someone had abducted Stacey.

The three law-enforcement officers shook hands.

Calvani asked, "What's the easiest way to get back to my car?"

"We'll go with you." Aragon took the lead. "We're going back to our vehicles too." He pointed the way toward the narrow road that led to the next street and parking area. They crossed two more before reaching Seagull.

Doug let the dog handler and Aragon go ahead while he called in to the dispatcher. "Let me speak to the chief please."

He described what had happened with the dog. The chief expressed his disappointment and sympathy and told Doug to come to the station. "We're expecting an FBI agent fairly soon and he'll want to talk to you."

Before following the others, Doug walked around the parking area. He knew if Stacey had been able, she'd have left a clue for him, but he didn't see anything. No torn pieces of material, no buttons, no bread crumbs. Possibly one of the neighbors had seen something. Right now, though, he was supposed to check into the station. When he had the opportunity, he'd ask Aragon to do the canvassing.

■

Tanner Benedict wasn't what anyone expected. Dressed in a dark blue suit, white shirt, and conservative tie, at first glance Abel thought the FBI agent looked like a salesman. He was young, early to mid-thirties, clean-shaven with a slight tan. On second thought, the man's sandy crew-cut and rigid posture suggested a military background.

This was the first time Abel had been in on an investigation with the FBI. He couldn't remember a time when Rocky Bluff P.D. had called the FBI about a case.

Along with Benedict, Lieutenant Stafford, Detective Marshall, Felix Zachary, a distraught and disheveled Doug Milligan gathered in Chief McKenzie's office. Extra chairs had been brought in to accommodate the group. Doug didn't sit, instead he ran his hands through his hair and paced the floor, leaving a fine trail of sand on the worn carpet.

After the chief introduced the FBI agent and explained what they knew so far about the missing officer, obviously puzzled, Benedict asked, "May I ask why everyone is so dressed up?"

Chief McKenzie tipped his head toward Doug.

Doug paused in his pacing long enough to say, "Stacey and I were getting married this morning. Everyone who was off-duty planned to attend along with their families. Now, they've all come in to help find Stacey."

"That explains it." Benedict smiled. "The reason I'm here is because there are some similarities between this case and others involving missing women I've been working on."

"Describe the similarities," McKenzie prompted.

"All the other women disappeared from small beach communities similar to this one. We have seven such cases ranging from the state of Washington to California. Whoever is responsible has been moving in a southerly direction. All of the missing women were small, 5' 4" or shorter, lived in a small coastal town, and most ran on the beach nearly everyday."

"Have you located any of them?" Stafford asked.

"No, I'm afraid we haven't." The agent stared at Doug.

Doug's expression changed from worried to stricken. "Oh, God."

"There are a couple of differences. Most of the women lived alone, but nothing appeared out of order inside their homes. They were punctual at their jobs until they went missing, and though all were responsible young women, some had left pets behind without any arrangements for their care. This fact alerted law enforcement that these women hadn't disappeared under their own volition." Benedict let his words sink in before going on.

Again he focused his attention on Doug. "Detective Milligan, I understand you were with the dog trainer and there was only minimal success."

Doug swallowed hard. "Yes, sir. The dog followed Stacey's scent from the beach to the closest parking spot where he lost it."

"Which I'm sure you've already surmised means she was abducted in a vehicle of some sort."

"Yes sir. Officer Aragon was with me. I gave him a call and asked him to canvass the neighborhood. He's now knocking on doors up and down that particular street to see if anyone noticed any unusual activity or cars they didn't recognize. What else can we do? What can I do?"

"Milligan, frankly I think it would be best if you stepped back and let the rest of us handle this case. Go home to your loved ones."

"I'm sorry. I can't do that. My loved one is the person who's missing."

"Understandable, but I'm going to be taking the lead and I expect that we can all work together with the same goal in mind, finding Stacey Wilbur and bringing her safely home."

The others made appropriate remarks. Abel peered at the chief, wondering how he felt about the FBI agent taking charge.

McKenzie's expression didn't change. "What should we do first?" If he wasn't pleased he didn't show it.

"I suggest you send another officer out to question people near the place where Officer Wilbur disappeared." He turned to Doug. "Was there anyone on the beach near where you found the sign of a struggle?"

Doug's face turned pale. "Yes, a couple of mothers with their kids."

The young FBI agent didn't look accusing as he continued, "I'm guessing by your expression you didn't talk to any of them to find if they'd seen anything suspicious."

Sand still clung to the bottoms of Doug's suit trousers. He'd shed his jacket and draped it over a chair. His tie was askew and his white shirt only half tucked in. "I did talk to one of the women. She said she didn't see anything. To be honest, my focus was on finding Stacey and keeping the place uncontaminated until the tracking dog arrived."

"Okay, Detective, if you want to continue with the search, my suggestion to you is to return to the place where the dog lost the scent, go to the beach and see if any of the people who were there when you arrived are still there. Question them again. They might remember seeing something unusual if you mention a strange vehicle in the vicinity." He smiled at Doug. "You know what to do."

Doug grabbed his suit jacket and left.

Agent Benedict continued, "What you want your people to be asking about is anyone who might be new in town. Probably someone who would blend into the background, an ordinary person no one paid any attention to. Ask about vehicles that have been cruising the beach areas. Our suspect is probably a psychopath and/or sociopath. These guys have no capacity for emotion. They don't feel shame, guilt or love. Usually they have a high I.Q. We've been after this guy for over three months and so far he hasn't left a clue. A suspect like this is hard to pinpoint because they imitate others and can be charming, even likeable. In the prior cases, we surmise the suspect presented himself to his other victims in ways that made him appealing."

The chief asked, "But Stacey would know better. She's smart too. She wouldn't go off with anyone, especially not today."

"No, I understand that. It's been a longer period of time since our last missing female was reported. Our thinking is the suspect is desperate. His need to abduct and do whatever he does to his victims has become overwhelming."

Chief McKenzie spoke up. "We've got a man at the TV station right now. Abel, would you get in touch with Strickland and make sure he's asking for information about any unusual activity, any new people or vehicles in the beach neighborhoods."

Knowing Ryan, Abel figured he'd already added that to the announcement, but he was happy to have something concrete to do. He couldn't imagine what Doug must be feeling right now.

■

All the way back to the beach, Doug's mind whirled. Why on earth hadn't he talked to the people on the beach? Vaughn could've protected the crime scene. Crime scene? At the time they were hoping it wasn't going to be one. The dog had proven it was. He couldn't allow his mind to imagine what Stacey might be going through. He'd never prayed much before, but now he begged God to protect Stacey.

He reached Sandpiper, the street where the dog had lost Stacey's scent. He parked the SUV that he'd bought to replace his MG, the car he'd planned to drive his new family in to Disneyland right after the wedding. He gulped hard.

He parked. He trudged to the top of the sand dune and peered down to scope the beach. The fog had lifted, leaving the sky a pale blue. Waves crashed. White foam raced toward the beach. The water, blue green near shore, became a deeper blue as it stretched toward the horizon. Since he'd left, more people had gathered to enjoy the unusually bright day. He wasn't sure he could pick out the family who'd been there earlier looking for Stacey.

He thought for a moment. When he first arrived, there'd only been one family on the beach. A mother with three children. They'd been fairly close to the place where it looked like there'd been a struggle.

The woman said she'd driven, so she must've parked on another street. He scanned the area again and spotted her. She wore dark glasses, shorts and a halter top. There were more children than he remembered. Another mother came from the water, with an additional child, both soaking wet. The second family had arrived after his conversation with the original mother. Three kids, two boys and a girl ran back and forth from the shoreline to where the first mother sat reading on a large red-white-and-blue striped towel.

When he approached, his shadow alerted her to his presence.

She turned, surprise in her expression quickly turned to recognition. "You're the policeman who was here earlier."

The wet mother stood nearby, toweling off and listening.

"Yes, ma'am."

"Did you find who you were looking for?" She laughed. "I guess not since you're back." She closed the paperback, her index finger keeping her place.

"I'd like you to think back to when you first arrived at the beach. Did you see anyone at all?"

"No, I'm sorry. I was concentrating on the kids."

"This is really important, ma'am. One of our female police officers came here to jog this morning and never returned home."

The woman frowned. "Oh, that's terrible, but I didn't see her or anyone else for that matter."

The oldest of her children, a boy of about seven came up and stared at Doug. His baggy shorts dripped sea water, sand stuck to his bare chest.

"Jeff, for goodness sake. Don't be rude. You'll have to excuse my son, he's terribly curious."

"Hi, Jeff." Doug leaned down and shook the boy's hand. "I'm looking for someone. Maybe you can help me. When you were coming to the beach this morning, did you see anyone around here? Or a car you've never seen before?"

Without hesitation, Jeff said. "A delivery van."

"Where did you see this delivery van?" Doug spoke calmly, trying not to let his hope rise.

"It's been here a bunch of times this week."

His mother sighed. "My son has a vivid imagination, Officer. You can never be sure if what he says is factual, or merely something he's dreamed up."

Jeff's face reddened. "It's true. I did see it. I saw it on the main street too, lots of times. And I saw it leaving the beach when we were coming down here." The boy crossed his arms over his skinny chest. "You never believe anything I say."

"That's because you make so much stuff up." She looked at Doug. "I wouldn't put too much faith in what..."

Doug interrupted her. "Jeff, what else can you tell me about this van? What color was it?"

The boy shrugged and stared at the sand. "I dunno. Kind of yellow, that's all. I think the driver wore sun glasses."

Jeff's mother rolled her eyes.

"Did you notice if there was any writing on the van? Maybe on the side?"

Another shrug. "Maybe."

"What about the license plate? Did it look like the license plate on your mom's car?"

"I dunno."

"Anything else you can tell me? It's really important."

The boy stood on one foot, and scratched his leg with the other. He glanced at his mother, then back at Doug. "It was like those yellow vans that used to deliver stuff. Once one of those vans brought a package to my mom."

"So it was medium sized, not as big as a brown UPS truck?"

"Uh huh."

Doug reached out and ruffled the boy's hair. "Thank you, Jeff, you've been very helpful."

"Who are you looking for?" he asked.

His mother grabbed him and pulled him down beside her. "Jeff, don't be so nosy."

"It's okay, ma'am. I'm looking for a lady police officer. She's my fiancé and we are supposed to get married today."

The mother wrinkled her brow. "Oh, I'm so sorry."

"You still have my card, right?"

"Yes, I put it in my pocket."

"If Jeff thinks of something else, no matter how far-fetched you think it might be, please call me right away."

One of her younger children was knocked down by a wave and screamed. She jumped to her feet. "I've got to go." She ran off toward the little girl who'd been dragged backwards onto the sand by what was probably her middle son.

Jeff said, "I hope you find her, mister."

"Me too."

Doug could feel the boy's gaze on him as he hurried back to his car. This was the first real clue—at least he hoped it was a real clue and that the mother's warning about her son's imagination wouldn't come back to haunt him. It gave him hope because he could remember when he was a kid and how curious he was and the things he noticed that no one else seemed to. When he mentioned what he'd seen, like Jeff, no one believed him if anyone bothered to listen.

He flipped open his phone and dialed the department. "Tell everyone to be on the look out for a medium-sized yellow delivery van."

CHAPTER 16

IT BECAME OBVIOUS the bride and groom-to-be weren't going to show up for their wedding. Guests who weren't married to police personnel began to wander around, not knowing what they should do, whispering among themselves. Of course, Stacey's disappearance had been announced earlier. Before the news had time to settle, Reverend Cookmeyer had led them in a prayer for her safety and quick return. The somber atmosphere in the church was more like a funeral than a celebration.

Clyde Osborne stood and addressed the crowd. "If all had gone like we'd expected, everyone would now be in the fellowship hall for the reception. Friends, there's a lot of good food waiting to be eaten. We really don't want it to go to waste."

His wife stood beside him, she brushed a tear from her cheek. "Yes, please come and eat. We'll all feel better if we have something in our stomachs."

Davey pulled on his grandmother's arm. "But what about Mommy? What is she going to eat?"

Clara Osborne's lips quivered and her eyes filled with tears. She grabbed her grandson's hand. "We'll save some for her, honey." To the others who watched her as though mesmerized, she said, "Please, we'd like to share this meal with you." She turned and headed for the side door.

Most of the people who'd been waiting for news of Stacey, followed Davey and Clara, though a few turned the other way and started for the main entrance.

Barbara Strickland and her three sons followed the Osbornes. Philip, the youngest asked, "Why don't you call Ryan and see if he knows anything. I feel sorry for Davey."

Barbara squeezed Philip's shoulder. "I feel sorry for all of them. When we get inside, why don't you sit with Davey? Maybe you can get his mind on something else besides his mom."

■

Ryan made his public statement on TV about Stacey's disappearance. Her police department photo was displayed along with her physical description. When Doug got in touch with Ryan about the yellow delivery van the boy had seen, he made another announcement asking for people to be on the look out for a yellow van, and if anyone saw it to call a specific number.

Rocky Bluff was small enough that if the yellow van was still around, surely someone would notice it. The problem was, it might not be in the area. If the person, no doubt a man, had a plan in mind when he snatched Stacey, surely part of that plan would be to get out of town as quickly as possible. Could be, though, that because the only way out of Rocky Bluff was the 101 freeway, the kidnapper had decided to hole up somewhere locally. Maybe, just maybe, there hadn't been much of a plan. That could be a good thing.

Ryan's cell phone rang. He flipped it open. "Strickland."

It was Barbara. "Any news?"

"They think she was taken in a small yellow delivery van. Of course everyone is out looking. The CHP has been alerted, and they'll be checking the freeways."

"Is there a chance it'll be found?"

"I certainly hope so. Depends upon a lot of variables."

"Like what?" Barbara prompted.

Ryan knew his wife was frustrated by his short answers. "If the kidnapper knew what he was doing, exactly where he was going, and headed there as soon as he snatched Stacey." One more thought popped into his brain. "All of this depends upon whether the tip about the yellow van is even valid."

"Oh, Ryan, why do you say that?"

"Barb, the information came from a kid. He didn't see Stacey being put into the van, or even see her in it. He just saw a van leaving the beach about the time Stacey might have disappeared."

Barbara was quiet for a moment. "That's all you have to go on?"

"Afraid so. All we know for sure is Stacey is missing. We think she was grabbed at the beach and taken away in a vehicle. We don't really know what kind of vehicle, but this is all we have right now."

"Holy Mary, Mother of God," came out in a rush. "This is worse than I thought. We better all pray even harder."

"You do that because we need a miracle."

"That's exactly what I'll pray for."

■

Still in his good suit, Gordon Butler waited at home for news about Stacey. The first time Doug called, he told Gordon to sit tight until he heard from him again. He continued watching TV in an effort to take his mind off what might have happened to Stacey. It wasn't too long ago he'd actually imagined that Stacey might fall for him. Of course, it didn't happen that way, but he had a lot of respect for her and could honestly say he was happy she and Doug had fallen in love. Both of them were good friends.

The TV show he'd been watching was interrupted by a special report. Ryan Strickland appeared on the screen. When Ryan showed Stacey's photo and stated where she'd last been seen, it became all too real. Stacey Wilbur had fallen into evil hands.

Gordon dashed up the stairs, shedding his jacket on the way. He yanked off his shirt, tie and trousers and discarded them on his bedroom floor. In record time, Officer Butler donned his uniform and all the required police paraphernalia and set off to help find Stacey.

■

A large map of Rocky Bluff had been divided into sectors. Some men had already been assigned areas to search. Others were on walking detail, questioning people and personnel in all the stores along Valley Boulevard. Gordon mentally chastised himself for waiting so long to report in. He'd hoped he'd still have the chance to serve as best man.

Someone Gordon had never seen before seemed to be in charge. The stranger identified himself as F.B.I. Agent Tanner Benedict. He didn't look old enough to be an F.B.I. agent, far too fresh-faced and innocent, nor did he resemble any portrayed on TV. If the man was type-cast, Gordon would have voted for a desk jockey of some sort or maybe a teacher fresh out of college. He certainly seemed self-assured. Gordon shook his hand and introduced himself, adding, "I'm good friends with the missing woman and her fiancé."

About the same height as Gordon, Agent Benedict peered directly at him. "I take it you're familiar with Rocky Bluff and its surroundings."

"Yes, sir."

"Looking at this map, can you think of any place we haven't sent someone yet, where you'd be willing to look either for the yellow van or someone who has seen it?"

Gordon moved close to the map and pointed to the southern end of the city limits bordered by the ocean. "Anyone gone to the campground?"

"No one mentioned it to me. You want to do that?" Benedict asked.

"Sure."

Gordon left immediately. When he went into the parking lot behind the station, he was shocked to see that though there were plenty of civilian vehicles, no police cars were available. Didn't matter. He'd use his own. Maybe he could grab an official car available later.

Even during winter months, the campground attracted RVers but only a few tent campers. Its location beside the ocean between Ventura and Santa Barbara made it a popular stopping off-place for some, and a vacation destination for others, even though it was more expensive than near-by state camping spots.

Gordon drove his Chevrolet sedan through the main entrance and parked next to the log cabin that was the office and owner's residence. Rayburn Nutting, an ex-biker, inherited money from his grandmother and invested it in the beach property that he'd developed into the triple A—rated camping facility.

Nutting popped his head out the front door and squinted as Gordon got out of his car. He waved a skinny, heavily tattooed forearm. His one gold earring glinted in the afternoon sunlight. "Officer, what can we do for you this fine day?" Since he'd left his biking days behind and turned entrepreneur, his pony-tail and handlebar mustache had turned white.

Gordon shook Nutting's offered hand. "Have you heard about Officer Wilbur's disappearance?"

"It's all over the news. I liked that young lady."

Gordon cringed at Nutting's use of past tense.

The man continued on, "She's been out here several times. Helped find some missing kids, took care of a few fights. She's all right, little but mighty." His voice sounded like he's smoked too many cigarettes far too long.

"Has anyone suspicious or out of the ordinary stayed here lately?"

Nutting guffawed which turned into a cough. When he finally stopped coughing, he said, "Lots of out of the ordinary camp here, as for the other, depends upon what you mean by suspicious."

Gordon said, "You know, a person alone, not in a motor home or fifth-wheeler."

"Driving a yellow delivery van."

Excited and hopeful, Gordon asked, "Did you see one?"

"Sorry. Wish I had."

"Anything at all?"

Nutting smoothed his mustache. "I don't know if this has anything to do with what you want to know, but the last couple of nights, after I closed the office, I heard a vehicle driving in. I planned to get their money in the morning. When I got up and drove around the park, whoever it was had gone. Happens from time-to-time. Cheapskates come in really late and bug out before I can catch 'em."

"But you didn't see whoever it was?" Could very well have been the yellow delivery van, but there was no way to prove it.

"Sorry, man, wish I knew more. Guess it's time I put in a video camera."

Gordon said, "Be a good idea. Thanks for your time."

He decided to go back to the station, hoping someone had returned one of the police cars. If he spotted the yellow van, it would be impossible to stop it without sirens and lights. He felt sick to his stomach about Stacey. He didn't want to consider what might be happening to her.

CHAPTER 17

THE AFTERNOON TRUDGED on with no news about or from Stacey. People were questioned up and down all the beach streets and in all the businesses on Valley Boulevard, but not a single person remembered seeing any strangers or a yellow delivery van. The police drove up and down every street in Rocky Bluff. Abandoned buildings were searched. No sightings of the yellow van had been reported in or around the beach community.

Doug's stomach knotted with fear. He didn't know what else he could do. Just when he'd thought his life was moving along in the right direction, it had taken a jolting swerve. He couldn't even think about what might be happening to Stacey. Horrible thoughts popped in and out of his mind. What would he do without her? Was she still alive? She had to be, or he'd know it, wouldn't he? Surely a loss so devastating would be something he'd feel in his soul. And if she was still alive, what was happening to her? Was she afraid? Was she suffering at the hands of some monster? Oh, God, please. No.

Unable to think straight, Doug returned to the police station, hoping that someone would have news. Good news. He didn't think he could handle the other kind.

FBI Agent Benedict continued to preside over the map on the wall and the men who moved in and out of the large room used for training, change of shift meetings, and various other activities. Filled with chairs, white boards, and other paraphernalia, at the moment only the agent and Chief McKenzie were present when Doug walked in.

He only heard the last of Benedict's sentence. "...if we haven't found her by nightfall, we probably won't find her at all."

It felt like an icy hand gripped Doug's heart.

Both men turned to look at him, pity evident in their expressions. "Any luck?" McKenzie asked though he obviously knew the answer.

"No, I've looked everywhere I could think of. I don't know what else to do." Doug knew he sounded like he was giving up, but that was far from the truth. "I hope everyone isn't focusing on trying to find a yellow van. The mother of the little boy who told me about it didn't think he was reliable."

"We've made it clear they should be looking for any suspicious vehicles or persons." The chief sounded reassuring though Doug wasn't sure that's what was happening.

"Our biggest hope is that the suspect hasn't left town. It's quite possible he's decided not to travel until dark. Less likelihood of being spotted." Benedict didn't look at Doug. Instead he focused on the map with all the pins stuck in it. "As you can see, the men have covered every area of Rocky Bluff."

"I know. I've been down most of those streets myself." Weariness settled over Doug. Not knowing what to do next was nearly as unsettling as not knowing what had happened to Stacey.

"Why don't you go see how Officer Wilbur's parents and her son are doing?" Chief McKenzie suggested. "I bet they'd like hearing a progress report from you."

Doug sighed. "What kind of progress should I give them? We can't find any trace of their daughter? We don't even have a clue as to where she might be? I don't think they want to hear that."

Still speaking in a kindly manner, the chief said, "I think you could put a more positive spin on what's happening. Let them know every man in the department is out looking for Officer Wilbur. We're using every available resource in our search."

"Since that does nothing to reassure me, I don't think it's going to reassure Mr. and Mrs. Osborne either, or Davey." Overwhelmed, Doug sunk into the nearest chair.

Chief McKenzie stepped closer to Doug and put a hand on his shoulder. "Maybe not, but I think seeing you might help them. Being with them could help you too."

Doug wanted to do something, anything to help find Stacey. The problem was he couldn't think of anything he hadn't already done. Maybe seeing her parents was a good idea. He rose. "I'll go. If anything comes up, anything at all, please call me on my cell."

"Of course," Agent Benedict said.

The phone rang. Chief McKenzie answered.

Doug paused.

The chief waved him away and shook his head.

Doug studied McKenzie's face, but his expression revealed nothing. Doug knew he was dismissed.

■

Agent Benedict didn't want anyone to know how much he felt Detective Milligan's pain. He'd just been married two days before he was assigned to the case of the missing women and hadn't been home since. He couldn't imagine how horrifying it would be to know that the woman you loved was at the mercy of a psychopath.

Benedict knew that police departments weren't always thrilled when the FBI came in to take over. In this instance, he hoped everyone felt like they were working as a team. The men in the department knew much more about the town's layout and potential hiding spots than he did, making them the logical ones to do the physical searching. Of course he was reporting regularly to his boss, but no new suggestions were forthcoming.

The truth was, he didn't feel hopeful about the outcome of this disappearance either. Unfortunately, most female victims were so terrorized they didn't fight back. He hoped this time might be different since this particular female happened to be a police officer. Whether or not the person who'd taken Wilbur was the kidnapper as in the prior cases, he probably had no idea who he'd abducted. This could work in Wilbur's favor unless somehow he discovered her identity.

On the other hand, if the suspect was the same person who'd nabbed the other missing women, the guy was smart enough to have gotten away with the other kidnappings without leaving trace of evidence behind. Because serial killers tended to be mobile, the only way to catch one was to follow his trail. Since no bodies had been discovered, there wasn't anything to track or many clues to follow.

■

Doug called Clyde Osborne's cell and learned, even though it was nearly dark, the family continued to wait at the church for news. By the number of cars still in the parking lot, Doug realized many others stayed with them.

He found everyone gathered in the sanctuary sitting in the first pews, though some knelt on the steps leading to the pulpit. It was obvious many prayed. His approach brought most heads turning toward him. Clyde Osborne rose quickly.

Before anyone could ask, Doug said, "I'm afraid I have nothing to report. The whole police force is out looking, but no one has come up with anything yet."

Clara Osborne pressed her lips together and wiped tears away with the back of her plump hand. "Oh, Doug. This is so terrible." She rose and met him in the aisle. She took his hands and squeezed.

Doug glanced around but didn't see Davey.

Before he could ask, Clara said, "Barbara Strickland took our grandson to her house. We figured the boys could keep him distracted."

"Good idea. This has to be scary for him too."

"It is, but he thinks his mother has super powers and has the ability to take care of herself no matter what."

Clyde joined them. "I want to think that too."

"Have you had anything to eat?" Clara asked.

Doug shook his head.

"Come with us into the fellowship hall. We sent some of the food to the homeless shelter, but we kept enough to snack on for those who are remaining here to pray for Stacey." Clara tucked her arm into the crook of Doug's elbow and maneuvered him toward the side door.

Once they'd entered the large room with tables still decorated for the wedding reception, Doug said, "I don't think I can eat."

"You have to keep up your strength. No telling what you'll be faced with as the night progresses," Clyde said while his wife went into the kitchen.

Doug studied the older man's face and could tell by the worry and fear in his eyes that he realized what the outcome could be.

■

Slowly, Stacey recovered consciousness but had no idea where she was.

Her head ached. For that matter her whole body ached. She groaned and blinked her eyes. Wherever she was, it was dark. She could tell she was in a vehicle of some sort, but she had no idea what kind. It smelled odd. Old and yet new. She also picked up the scent of stale French Fries which brought on a sudden hunger pang, but fear immediately replaced that sensation.

She shifted her position. Rope dug into her flesh. Her hands were tied behind her back. She wriggled her wrists, but the bond was tight.

Horrible thoughts flooded her brain. She fought back the panic that started to take over, she needed to think clearly.

The last thing she remembered was running on the beach, her mind filled with wonderful expectations of the day to come and her long-anticipated wedding to Doug. Poor Doug. He must be frantic. She wondered what happened at the church when she didn't show up. Her poor folks. And Davey, what must he be thinking? Oh, dear God, would she ever see Davey again?

This was her own fault. She hadn't been paying attention while she ran or this never could've happened. Why did she let her guard down? Because she knew the man who'd been exposing himself was in jail.

Whoever did this knew what he was doing. Obviously he'd done it before. He'd managed to sneak up on her and strike her over the head hard enough to keep her unconscious for most of the day. At least she felt like it was most of the day. In reality, she had no way of knowing how much time had passed.

It was dark, or at least inside wherever she was it was dark. She seemed to be alone. She couldn't hear anything. No sounds of anyone shifting around. No breathing, except for her own.

Time to quit wondering about what had happened, and see if she could manage to get away. Her legs were free. Whoever had taken her was pretty sure of himself, or at least expected her to remain unconscious until his return. She pulled against the ropes binding her wrists. They bit into her flesh, but there was the tiniest bit of give. She wiggled her wrists some more. Maybe if she could get her arms in front, she could use her teeth to untie the knots.

She rolled over onto her side. Bending her knees, she folded her legs tight against her chest. Maneuvering slowly, she shifted her weight, trying to pull her arms down over her bottom and then up over her feet and her legs. Her first attempt didn't work.

Knowing that success could mean the difference between life and death, she concentrated as she moved slowly and finally pulled her arms over her feet and bent legs until her arms were in front of her body. Her eyes had adjusted a bit to the darkness. She could see the rope around her wrists was narrow, but circled several times. The knot was in front of her. It looked secure and not something she'd easily be able to work free even if she had full use of her hands.

She tried pulling her wrists apart. They moved a fraction of an inch. She did it again, but nothing changed.

Feeling frantic, because she had no idea how much time she had before her captor returned, she tried to think what else she could do that might loosen her bond.

She leaned over and spit directly on her wrists. Working her hands back and forth, spitting, pulling, over and over, she thought she might actually be able to free herself. And if she did, she knew she could escape.

Her spirits rose. She had a chance of getting away.

One wrist slid a tiny bit under the rope. She spat again and pulled. One hand slid about an inch.

Gathering as much spittle as possible, she spit on the same place.

With a big yank, her hand came free. Then the other. She let the rope drop and crawled on her knees. She needed to figure out how to make her escape. She felt around. There didn't seem to be anything she could use as a weapon.

The sound of a heavy shoe or boot crunching on gravel alerted her. Oh, God, whatever she was going to do had to be accomplished in a hurry. Her captor had returned.

■

Doug returned to the station, but there wasn't any news. He wondered why there was only one FBI agent on the case, but he had to admit, Benedict seemed to know what he was doing. Doug wished he knew what to do. Despite everyone being on the lookout for a yellow van, or any suspicious vehicles, no one had come up with anything. Plenty of cars, vans and trucks had been stopped, but no clues to Stacey's whereabouts had been discovered.

Of course there was always the possibility that it was only a long-shot that Stacey's disappearance had anything to do with the other women's disappearances. That might be why Benedict was the only FBI agent here.

If Stacey could, she would've called. Doug knew she wouldn't remain passive. She knew the only way for a victim in this kind of situation to save her life was to fight back. Stacey was either incapacitated or...he couldn't allow himself to complete that thought.

Agent Benedict seemed to notice Doug staring at the white board where all the information they'd gathered so far was written. As far as he could tell, even though there was an abundance of writing, nothing seemed to be helpful.

"I'm glad you're here, Detective. I've got a few questions for you."

"Ask away." Doug couldn't think of anything he hadn't already offered on his own.

"Did Stacey have any women friends she liked to hang out with? Someone we could question who might know something that was troubling her?"

Doug fought to remain calm. "Nothing was troubling her. She was excited about our wedding. She could hardly wait for this day to arrive."

Benedict nodded. "I understand that, but please answer my question."

What question? Oh. "No, she didn't hang out with any women friends. She was a police officer who specialized in investigating vice crime. We don't have any other female officers on the force, if we did she might be friends with them. You know how difficult it is to be friends with someone who isn't in police work. Besides, she's the mother of a six-year old and likes to spend time with him. I have to repeat what I said before, nothing was troubling her. If there were, I'd have been the first one she'd tell."

The FBI agent studied him, his stare penetrating as though he could make Doug confess. Doug had certainly used the same technique himself plenty of times, in an effort to unnerve a suspect.

Swell, now that meant Benedict considered Doug a suspect. Since they couldn't find anyone else, no wonder he was now in the running. But if the agent concentrated on him, that could decrease efforts in finding whoever actually had Stacey. He had to convince Benedict he didn't have anything to do with her disappearance.

"Look, Agent Benedict, I know you want to put an end to this case. Maybe you've decided there's no link between Stacey's disappearance and the other cases you've been investigating and you're probably anxious to move on. But I need you to understand something. I love Stacey with all my heart. I had no idea she was missing until her parents called me. She didn't let me know she planned to go jogging on the beach this morning, or I'd have talked her out of it."

Doug took a deep breath before continuing. "I don't want Stacey to be a victim of whoever it is you've been tracking, but if she is, I want you to put all your effort and expertise into locating her. Focusing on me would be a terrible waste of time. I have a horrible feeling wasting time is not a good thing to do right now." Doug was surprised Benedict didn't interrupt his speech.

Actually, the agent's expression softened a bit while Doug spoke.

"To be perfectly frank, Detective," Benedict said, "I'm running out of ideas here. Unless one of the officers in the field happens to find something, or run across a suspicious character or vehicle, I'm afraid we're fast approaching a dead end."

Doug's heart sank.

■

CHAPTER 18

GORDON BUTLER FELT better now that he had a regulation police car to drive. If he spotted a suspicious vehicle at least he would have lights and a siren to use. He imagined coming across the yellow delivery van, turning on his siren and chasing down the kidnapper. He would leap out of his car, gun in hand, jerk the driver's door open, slam him against the hood with legs spread, handcuff him and put him on the ground for back-up to take care of. He'd rescue Stacey from inside the van and he'd be a hero.

He was so caught up in his day-dream, he nearly ran over an old lady with a shopping cart in a crosswalk on Valley Boulevard. She jumped out of the way of his front bumper and glared at him.

He rolled down his window and shouted, "I'm sorry."

She shouted back, "You should be," and stomped her way to the curb.

Oh boy. He better get his head on straight or he wouldn't be any use to Stacey or anyone else. He decided to drive up and down the streets leading to Valley Boulevard. He'd done that once already, but it wouldn't hurt to double check. It was nearly dark. If the person who'd grabbed Stacey was still in town, he'd probably be making his move soon.

■

Vaughn Aragon felt weary. Not so much because of Stacey Wilbur's disappearance but because of all the hours he'd been putting in. Earlier he'd been assigned to walk up and down Valley Boulevard, going into each retail store and restaurant asking people if they'd noticed any suspicious newcomers, or any strangers at all, but no one saw anything helpful.

He'd asked Sergeant Navarro, who had been on duty since being notified of Officer Wilbur's disappearance, if he and Zachary should be on hand for the nightly gathering in front of the furniture store. Though finding Wilbur was top priority, when it started to get dark, Navarro wanted Zachary and Aragon to return to their regular crowd control assignment.

Zachary and another officer had been stationed at the on-ramp to the freeway watching all vehicles leaving the area. So far they'd seen nothing suspicious though they had stopped a few vans and trucks.

Though disappointed, Aragon's gut feeling was what they were all doing was nothing but a waste of time. Whoever took Wilbur had left the area before anyone even knew she was gone. She was probably already dead. Not an easy thing to consider. He sighed. Although he didn't know her all that well, besides Zachary, he'd interacted with her more than anyone else. He sighed again. Hell of a thing to happen to someone right before her wedding.

As far as he was concerned, the whole lot of them were literally spinning their wheels as they covered the same ground over and over. No one had found anything to suggest Wilbur and her captor were still in Rocky Bluff. It was as though Stacy had evaporated. As each hour passed, the likelihood of finding her alive lessened.

The street lights had come on. He decided to take a quick bathroom break before heading to the place where the angel in the window beguiled so many people.

■

Felix Zachary stopped by his house to check on Wendy. As soon as he pulled in front, Wendy came running out the door. She still had on the outfit she'd donned for the wedding. Her blonde hair flowed behind her as she hurried toward him.

After he got out of the car, she asked, "Any news?"

He embraced her, her protruding belly preventing him from drawing her as close as he'd like. "No, nothing."

Wendy frowned. "That's not good, is it?"

"No, it isn't."

"Poor Stacey. Poor Doug." She pulled away from him. "Have you eaten anything?"

"Not since breakfast."

"I have hot soup on the stove and made sandwiches. Why don't you come in for awhile?"

He used his radio to call in requesting a dinner break and got it. He could tell by the dispatcher's voice, she was tiring too. Everyone was working a double shift, some came in from a day off.

"She's letting me have half an hour, but then Navarro wants me to go back to the furniture store for crowd control. Might as well, I suppose, we haven't found any clues that might lead us to Stacey."

"Come inside. Tell me what's been going on." She took his hand.

For a moment, his mind flitted to thoughts of Doug Milligan. How on earth was the man coping? He couldn't imagine how he'd feel if Wendy was the one missing.

■

Abel Navarro moved between the command post the chief and FBI Agent Benedict had set up and the dispatchers' station. He talked to the men in the field via radio and in-person when they came into the station.

He was surprised when Maria called him on his cell phone. "I'm right outside. Juan's wife is taking care of Lupita. I've brought your dinner. I knew you wouldn't have a chance to come home."

The receptionist buzzed Maria inside and Abel met her in the hall. She carried a plate with foil over the top.

He kissed her cheek. "Thanks, honey. I didn't realize how hungry I was until you called. Smells good. What is it?"

"Chili rellenos, beans and rice. Tortillas too, of course. I even made a green salad."

"Come with me to my desk. Sit with me while I eat."

"Of course. I figure I won't have much opportunity to see you until Stacey's found."

He settled behind his desk and unwrapped his dinner. Maria pulled up a chair across from him. He crossed himself and blessed the food. "It's going to be awhile, that's for sure."

"Are there any leads yet?"

He scooped beans into a tortilla and took a big bite. After he chewed for a moment, he said, "Not really. It's like she vanished into thin air."

"Didn't you tell me an FBI man is here?"

"He's here, but he doesn't know any more than we do." Abel ate some of the rellenos.

Maria wrinkled her nose. "Why is he here then?"

"Don't repeat this, but he thinks Stacey's disappearance may be linked to some other women who are missing from small beach towns like ours."

"That doesn't sound good."

"You're right, it doesn't." While they talked, he continued eating even though he felt a twinge of guilt enjoying his food while Stacey was missing.

"I've always heard you say if it takes too long to solve a crime, it might never get solved."

"True."

"What will the department do if you can't find her?"

"We'll never give up. After awhile, we'll just scale down the investigation."

Maria stared at him for a long moment. "Until you find her," she paused again and swallowed hard, "one way or another."

He nodded. He knew she didn't want to say "until you find her body" and he didn't want to think that either.

■

In the Strickland household the late afternoon passed fairly smoothly. The boys kept Davey busy with video games and other pursuits. Philip brought out the Legos he hadn't played with for a couple of years. He and Davey built a humongous apparatus Philip identified as a space station.

When it grew dark, Barbara made toasted cheese sandwiches and tomato soup. While Davey was eating, a tear slid down beside his nose. "My mom always makes me sandwiches like this."

Barbara's three boys, usually noisy during meals, didn't speak. She had a feeling they were remembering a time, not so long ago, when their father hadn't come home.

Davey pushed away the plate with his half-eaten sandwich. "I want to go home." His lower lip quivered.

"Okay, honey, I'll call your grandparents."

After several rings, Clyde Osborne picked up the phone. "Yes?"

Immediately, Barbara knew by the sound of his voice he thought he'd be hearing news about his daughter. “Mr. Osborne, this is Barbara Strickland. Davey would really like to come home.”

“Could you please let me talk to him?”

“Of course.” She was surprised to see Davey already standing beside her. She handed him the phone.

“Grandpa, is Mommy home yet?”

Davey listened quietly and he sniffled. His eyes filled with tears. “No. I want to come home. When Mommy comes home, she’ll want me to be there.”

The little boy nodded. “Okay.” He handed the phone back to Barbara. “My Grandpa’s coming to get me.”

“Why don’t you finish your supper until he gets here.”

“No, I’ll wait by the door.”

She knew arguing with him wouldn’t change his mind. She smiled and smoothed his hair.

Davey ran to the couch and he knelt on the cushions and peeked out through the drapes at the street.

Barbara’s heart ached for the little boy. She prayed he wouldn’t have to experience what her own sons had gone through.

CHAPTER 19

THE SOUND OF footsteps grew louder as someone approached the back of the truck. Maybe someone to rescue her? Nice thought, but Stacey knew it wasn't true.

She moved closer to the end of the vehicle. She'd decided it was a delivery vehicle, but there was something odd about it. If this was the cargo compartment, it wasn't as big as a van.

One thing she hoped was whoever had taken her captive expected her to still be unconscious with her hands tied. At least, she'd have the advantage of surprise, when the door opened.

She fought to keep calm, not an easy task. She breathed slowly and deeply, concentrating on her heartbeat. Slow. Steady.

She'd been taught that relaxed energy was more powerful than hard energy and could be more effective against a stronger adversary. It would be easier if she were under the person's center of gravity, but that probably wasn't going to be the case.

The door handle squeaked as it turned. Stacey sat close, facing the door, with her knees drawn up.

When the door opened, she could see that it was nighttime, but still lighter outside than in the van. She didn't take the time to notice any other details, except the man in front of her was tall and slim, with a hood on his head and pulled down to his brow.

His eyes popped open as Stacey exploded toward him with both feet aimed toward his mid-section. He made an "Ooomph" sound as the air was driven out of his belly. He staggered backwards.

Immediately, she launched herself out of the vehicle. Using both hands, with all her strength and weight behind her, she connected with his chest. This wasn't how she'd been taught in her tai chi class, but it was effective. The man lost his balance and fell backward onto his butt. She landed on top of him.

Stacey scrambled to her feet and started running. She barely paused to look at the vehicle she'd been held captive in, but knew she'd need to be able to describe it when she found help. It wasn't like anything she'd ever seen before. It was an older model, combination van and station wagon, maybe a Ford, with a rather square shape. She couldn't really tell what color it was, greenish, maybe.

In seconds, she'd dashed past the vehicle and realized she was in an orange grove. She could smell the cloying sweetness of the blossoms. Orange groves covered the hills on the other side of the freeway from the city and the ocean. Maybe she could locate a farm house where she could call the police or find the road and flag down a motorist before her kidnapper recovered and caught his breath enough to come after her—which wasn't going to take him long.

Low clouds blocked the moon. A good thing, even though she couldn't see too far ahead, it meant neither could the kidnapper. She decided it would be best to crisscross through the rows of trees rather than run in a straight line, even though it would take longer to find help—but it also would be harder for him to track her down. Oh, how she wished for her cell phone.

One thing she did know was to head downhill toward Rocky Bluff.

A horrifying thought struck her. What if she wasn't in Rocky Bluff any longer? She had no idea how long she'd been unconscious. Judging by the night sky, she presumed at least for all of the morning and afternoon and more—on what should have been her wedding day. What if it were longer?

While she'd been out, she had no idea where the man might have driven, how far or how long. There were orange groves all over this part of California. She could be anywhere.

Shaking her head in an effort to rid herself of negative thoughts, she tried hard to think. Her head really hurt, making it difficult to concentrate on anything other than getting away.

Whether still in Rocky Bluff or not, she needed to keep away from the man who'd been holding her and to find someone who could help.

Only minutes passed before she heard the pounding of footsteps behind her though off to the side.

Her heart beat quickened and seemed to echo in her brain. She put her hand on her chest as if to quiet it. Once she realized her pursuer wasn't right on her trail, she calmed a bit. Thankfully, her running shoes didn't make much noise as she zigzagged her way through the rows of orange trees. The air was filled with the sweet scent of the blossoms along with a tinge of rotting oranges beneath the trees. She thought she could detect an underlying salty trace of the ocean air. She prayed that wasn't merely wishful thinking.

Ahead of her, the grove ended next to what looked like a paved road. The kidnapper was too close for her to step into open space. Instead, she moved farther to the side, squatted down behind a thick trunk, and waited.

He ran past where she'd been and out into the open. She could see him peering one way and then another. Now she could take the time to make note of what he looked like. About five eight or nine. Slim. He pushed the hood back off his head. White. Sharp features. Deep set eyes. Light brown hair, neither short or long, but shaggy. His sweat shirt was open in front. Red plaid shirt underneath. Baggy work pants. Gray. Boots with scuffed toes. If she could reach safety, at least she now had a good description to relay.

He turned around and squinted back toward the orange grove.

Stacey tried to make herself smaller. Invisible.

He didn't act like he'd seen her. Standing in the middle of the road, he scratched his head.

Taking long strides, he started back into the orange grove, but he wasn't headed in her direction. She guessed he was going back to his vehicle. When she was sure he was out of sight, she stood and sprinted across the road and slid down into a gully.

She could hear cars passing on the freeway not too far off. She smiled, almost positive she was still in Rocky Bluff. Of course, she could be in any beach town with orange groves on the hillsides. She preferred to think she hadn't been taken far from where she'd been abducted. If correct, she even had a general idea of her location.

Her head ached. The back of her skull throbbed. She ignored the pain. Crouching, she moved as fast as possible in the gully running beside the road. If she was right, the off and on ramp of the freeway was nearby. A gas station with a mom-and-pop store was on the south-west corner. If she could make it there without being discovered, she could call for help.

A vehicle started up behind her. She ducked down, peering over the top of the gully. Headlights shone through the trees. The vehicle that she couldn't name roared out onto the road. The paint job looked new. Might be vintage. It seemed to be a cross between a sedan and a delivery van. She'd never seen anything like it before.

She ducked her head down as the car moved slowly past her hiding spot. When it passed, she kept low but moved faster toward the corner the van turned down. She needed to go the same direction.

Once she made it around the corner, she could see the gas station. The delivery sedan parked beside the entrance. The man climbed out and hurried inside.

She didn't stop. Though cautious, she jogged in that direction, watching for the man to come out of the store. When he did, his head turned this way and that, no doubt still trying to spot her. Once he was inside the vehicle, he started back up the hill. He probably figured she'd gone the other way when she left the orange grove.

Crouching, she hid behind a bush as he drove by.

Now close enough to the store, she knew that even if he spotted her in his rearview mirror, she could sprint to safety.

Standing, she glanced behind her. The red taillights continued to diminish until they disappeared. With a burst of energy, she dashed down the hill, legs moving as fast as she could go. Her heart pumped faster and faster. She raced past the gas pumps, ignoring the stares of the two customers putting gas in their cars.

She yanked open the door and ran inside.

A young Hispanic woman manned the counter. "Hey, you're the lady that man was in here asking about a few minutes...."

Stacey interrupted. "That man kidnapped me. I'm a police officer. I need to make a call." Leaning over the counter, she grabbed a phone out of the cradle.

The young woman gasped and her eyes grew huge.

After dialing 911, Stacey described the vehicle that she'd been held captive in and where she'd last seen it.

The dispatcher asked for her present location and she gave it.

Not wanting him to get away, she added, "The man who kidnapped me is still in the area."

The green delivery sedan buzzed past the mini-market.

"He's headed toward the freeway. Get someone after him now."

■

Though Felix Zachary wanted to continue searching for Stacey, he obeyed orders to monitor the crowd milling about in front of the angel in the window. Vaughn Aragon was with him. The crowd gathered had grown too large for one man to handle. Both would have preferred to be on patrol, to watch for any suspicious cars or people, anything that might lead to Stacey Wilbur's whereabouts.

■

Even though it was supposed to be Gordon Butler's day off, he wasn't about to quit looking for Stacey. He'd run into Doug at the station, and it seemed like his friend had given up hope. He'd never seen his roommate look so downcast.

He patted Doug's shoulder. "Hey, Milligan, don't worry. We're going to find her. I'm going back out to look for her now."

"Thanks, Gordon." A smile flickered and immediately faded. "If you see or hear anything, let me know right away, okay, buddy?"

"You'll be the first."

For all of his bravado, Gordon didn't really know where he ought to go. Seemed like he'd covered Rocky Bluff three or four times, and he knew his fellow officers had done the same.

Back in his patrol car, he decided he'd do what he always did when he didn't have a call, he headed out toward the freeway entrance.

Before he reached it, the radio buzzed and the dispatcher came on the air. "Be on the lookout for a delivery sedan. Light green in color. Reported to be the vehicle driven by Officer Wilbur's kidnapper."

What did that mean? Had Stacey been rescued? Where was she? Was she all right?

Gordon vaguely remembered a report of a stolen restored vintage Ford Falcon that the car collector called a delivery sedan. Was that the vehicle the dispatcher was talking about?

Before he could ask any questions, a sedan of that description sped by him.

Gordon turned on his lights, made a U-turn, trounced the gas pedal, and began his pursuit.

■

Doug was on his way out of the station when Agent Benedict hollered at him. "Detective."

What now? Had the FBI guy decided he was the primary suspect after all? Doug turned.

The big guy had a sappy grin on his face.

What was that all about? "Yeah?"

"Officer Wilbur is safe."

Doug's heart leaped in his chest. He wasn't sure whether to believe the news or not. "Where is she? Is she okay?"

"I don't know the details. The dispatcher has the location of her whereabouts. Don't you think you ought to be the one to get her? Take her to the hospital first, make sure she's all right. Then bring her in for me to debrief."

"Of course. I'll do whatever you say, but where is she?"

Before Agent Benedict finished giving the name and complete location of a well-known convenience store near the freeway entrance, Doug sprinted through the police station.

■

CHAPTER 20

IMMEDIATELY, THE DRIVER of the delivery sedan spotted Gordon's police car. The suspect had been headed toward the freeway entrance, but when Gordon approached in his blue-and-white, emergency lights flashing, the other car's tires squealed, made a U-turn and zoomed off toward town.

Gordon floored his accelerator and keyed his mike. After identifying himself, he said, "I'm in pursuit of the suspect's vehicle. Heading westbound on Tulip toward Valley Boulevard." He gained on the older model vehicle and came close enough to make out the license plate. He rattled off the number.

No surprise when the dispatcher came back on to tell him the vehicle was stolen. Butler beeped his horn and started his siren. Instead of slowing, the old Ford Falcon pulled away.

The stolen vehicle reached Valley Boulevard and sailed around the corner on two tires. For a moment it looked like it might tip over. Back on four wheels, it raced ahead of Butler's car.

He wished another police car would show up. Surely someone was out there who could join the chase. Everyone on the department had been cruising around looking for something or someone unusual, anything that would lead to Stacey's location. Where were they now?

Smoke billowed from behind the Falcon's tires. The suspect was trying to slow down—or at least that's what it looked like.

Gordon spotted the reason. Crowds of people spilled out into the street in front of the angel window. Oh no! Gordon feathered his brakes, slowing down.

People heard the siren and saw the headlights of the first car as it sped toward them. Faces registered horror. Eyes huge, mouths open, screaming perhaps, but Gordon could hear nothing over the sound of his siren. He recognized uniformed Felix Zachary trying to herd people out of harm's way. The crowd divided, some running one way, some another. Others zigzagged and changed directions.

Gordon couldn't believe what happened next.

■

Vaughn Aragon watched with disbelief. A greenish older model station wagon, an old Falcon maybe, sped toward them at a great rate of speed, tires smoking. The crowd parted like the Red Sea, everyone running in all directions trying to get out of the way. A police car followed in close pursuit.

The driver of the first vehicle bailed and landed hard on the ground. His car kept going.

People screamed as they darted this way and that. Zachary shouted, trying to get people to move toward the median. Parents yanked their children out of the way.

The Falcon veered to the right, barely missing folks on either side as it jumped the curb. With an enormous bang, the car plowed into the store. The window shattered. Pieces of glass showered the pavement. The angel was no more.

The driver moved slightly, then disappeared under the police car which came to a screeching halt.

"Oh, my God," Vaughn shouted over the din as he started running toward the police car.

Zachary came right behind him. "Who's in the police car?"

Vaughn could see the Gordon Butler inside. Ghostly pale, his eyes were enormous. Bending down, Vaughn expected to see a mangled body under the car. Instead, bloody hands reached out and grasped the front bumper of the police car. The driver of the Falcon pulled himself up and onto his feet. For one long moment, he stared through the windshield at Butler.

"Hey! Are you all right?" Vaughn hollered.

The man turned, stared at him, blinked twice and took off in a strange hopping run.

Butler came after this guy for a reason, Vaughn wasn't about to let him get away. "Stop," Vaughn shouted, but the injured suspect kept going with that curious hip-hop gait. Vaughn charged after him.

The man fled around the corner of the furniture store, Vaughn only a few feet behind him. "Halt! Police!"

The man dropped to his knees, yanked a gun from the back of his pants and pointed it at Vaughn.

Ducking behind the side of the building, Vaughn pulled his own service revolver.

Vaughn had his finger on the trigger, but he couldn't squeeze it.

The suspect shot. The sound echoed through the narrow alley between the two buildings.

Behind him, people screamed. Though Vaughn didn't look back, he knew the crowd cowered, dropping to the ground.

Vaughn peeked around the corner.

The man fired again.

Vaughn knew he should fire his own gun, but his finger froze on the trigger. He couldn't move.

Another shot rang out, this time from someplace behind him. He ducked again.

The suspect staggered backwards, grabbing his arm.

"Drop your gun," Zachary ordered.

The man released his weapon. It clunked to the ground. The man stepped backwards.

Zachary darted past Vaughn. "Cover me."

In seconds, Zachary had the man down on the ground, his hands behind his back and handcuffed. "Call it in, Aragon."

Approaching sirens let Vaughn know help was already on the way. He was so shaken, he couldn't speak.

Zachary had the guy back on his feet. Blood soaked through the sleeve of the man's hooded sweatshirt. Zachary led him past Vaughn and into the street.

Onlookers cheered.

Two more police cars rolled to a stop behind Butler's. The officers piled out along with Agent Benedict.

An ashen-faced Butler stood beside his patrol car.

“Who is this guy?” Zachary asked.

“Stacey’s kidnapper,” Butler said.

“Too bad you didn’t do more damage when your car ran over him,” Zachary said. “If I’d known who he was, I might have aimed for something more serious than his arm.”

“It’s good he’s still alive. The FBI will want to question him about the other missing women.” Butler’s voice sounded like Vaughn felt, shaken.

With long strides, Benedict joined the group. “Indeed we will.” He had a huge smile on his face.

“Someone call an ambulance. No matter what he’s done, he still needs medical treatment,” Zachary said.

An ambulance arrived in minutes. The attendants administered medical aid, put the suspect on a gurney, and lifted him into the back of the ambulance. Agent Benedict climbed in with him. “Someone let the chief know where I’m headed,” he shouted before the ambulance doors slammed shut.

“So, Butler, let us in on what’s going on,” Zachary said.

“Dispatch reported Stacey was safe, but she’d been abducted by a man in an older model station wagon. The license number came back as a stolen Falcon delivery wagon, the one I was chasing.”

With his thumb, Zachary pointed over his shoulder at the wrecked car. “I never saw a van like that before.”

“Me neither, but when I heard the description I remembered it from a stolen car report. I spotted the suspect’s vehicle almost immediately. When I started after him, he changed direction and drove down here.” Butler took a deep breath. “I was sure I’d killed him. Figured the body was mangled. Couldn’t believe it when the suspect crawled out and started running.”

“None of us could,” Zachary said.

Butler’s eyes bulged and his hands shook. “I’ve never been so scared in my whole life.”

Vaughn felt the same way. Freezing like he did meant the end of his job.

Butler shook his head. “I knew I should have gotten out and chased that guy, but I couldn’t move.”

Zachary patted Butler’s shoulder. “We got the guy and Wilbur’s safe. She is safe, right?”

"Sounds like it."

"That's all that matters. Come on, Aragon, let's get this crowd dispersed so we can get a tow truck out here and a crew to help clear this mess. It's going to be a long night."

No one seemed to notice that Vaughn hadn't said a word.

■

Doug checked out a police car, turned on the lights and sirens and sped toward the mini-market where Stacey waited. He'd never considered himself a praying man, but he'd sure done plenty of it since Stacey's disappearance. Now that she was safe, it was time to thank God.

Wild thoughts interrupted his exuberance about being reunited with her. Where had she been? What had happened to her during the time she was gone? Was she injured? Or, please God no, had she been raped?

He shook his head. No, nothing like that. If so, an ambulance would've been dispatched. As far as he knew, he'd been the only one told about her location. Agent Benedict turned out to be a better man than Doug had given him credit for. At least Doug wouldn't have to deal with the press or curiosity seekers—yet.

Doug sped north, paying scant attention to anything around him. He slowed but didn't stop for any traffic lights.

After what seemed an eternity, which in reality was less than fifteen minutes, he pulled right in front of the convenience store. When he didn't see Stacey immediately, his heart sank. He'd expected her to come running out to greet him. Had he gone to the wrong store? No, this was the address Agent Benedict had given him.

He leaped out of the car and dashed toward the entrance. Still no sign of Stacey. Inside, he displayed his badge. "I'm Detective Milligan here to pick up Officer Wilbur. She is here, isn't she?"

A young, slim Hispanic woman with abundant dark hair combed back into a pony tail, smiled. "Yes, sir, back here with me. She was feeling faint."

Doug leaned over the counter and saw Stacey huddled on the floor holding a baggie filled with ice against the back of her head. She smiled at him, but pain reflected in her eyes.

"Oh, my God, Stacey, you're hurt." He moved around the counter. "Let me take a look."

She lifted the ice, revealing a large lump. "I didn't even know I had this until after I called the station. Then I started feeling woozy and I had to sit down. My head aches like crazy. Guess I was running on adrenalin before." Despite being extremely pale with dark circles around her eyes, she looked beautiful to him.

"I'm taking you to the hospital."

"No, I want to see Davey and my folks. They need to know I'm all right."

"I'll let them know." He scooped her up in his arms. "You have to see a doctor. Likely you have a concussion."

She struggled a bit. "Really, I can walk."

"Doesn't matter, I've got you now." He turned to the young woman and grinned. "Thank you for taking care of her."

"It was nothing, sir. I'm just glad she's okay."

He carried her to the police car and carefully put her in the passenger seat. When he'd fastened her seat belt and slid in the driver's seat, he said, "Besides your head, is there anything else wrong?"

A tear ran down her cheek, followed by another and another. She cried, "Yes."

Doug's heart skipped a beat as he imagined the worst.

"I missed our wedding." She rubbed her wrists and then held up her left hand, and wailed even louder.

"Now what?"

"My engagement ring is gone. That horrible man must've taken it."

■

CHAPTER 21

BOTH STACEY AND her kidnapper were admitted as patients to Rocky Bluff Hospital. The kidnapper went to the operating room, for repair work on his arm and leg. A guard stood watch outside the door, while Agent Benedict hovered nearby.

After being checked in, Stacey put on a hospital gown; a nurse bagged her clothes. Despite her protests, after the X-ray of her skull was read, she was taken to a room.

Doug called Mr. and Mrs. Osborne who arrived within minutes with Davey in tow. On the floor where Stacey had been taken, a nurse tried to block their way. "Sorry, it's after visiting hours." She glanced at Davey. "Besides, no children under twelve are allowed on this floor."

"We're her parents. We've been so worried," Clyde Osborne said.

"Please." Clara peeked around the nurse. She held Davey by the hand.

Stacey could hear this exchange and called out, "Please, Doug, can't you do something?"

Doug stepped to the door, and spoke in a cajoling voice. "Please, nurse, can't you break the rule this once? Officer Wilbur has been through a lot today. She really needs to see her family."

Before he finished talking, Davey broke away from his grandmother's grasp, rushing past the nurse and Doug.

"Mommy, Mommy," he cried and leaped onto his mother's bed. He gave her a big kiss and Stacey hugged him tight.

The nurse sighed and stepped aside. "The patient really needs her rest, but she'll probably heal faster after she has the chance to see all of you. Go on in."

Despite her pounding head and the purple bruises and the raw abrasions around her wrists like thick bracelets, Stacey beamed. "Oh, Davey, I'm so glad to see you."

"Mama, you didn't come to the wedding."

"I know. A bad man kept me away."

"Grandma told me. Are you going to have another wedding?"

Doug moved closer to Stacey. "As soon as your mother is well enough." He squeezed her hand.

Clyde and Clara stood on the other side of the bed, worry still apparent in their expressions.

Clara smoothed her daughter's forehead. "Are you sure you're all right? The doctor told us you have a concussion."

"My head really hurts." She sniffled. "And my engagement ring is gone."

"Oh, honey," Clara said.

"We think the suspect took it." Doug caressed the finger that no longer displayed the ring he'd given her.

"Maybe we should all clear out of here and let you get some rest," Clyde said, though he didn't look like he wanted to leave.

"No, don't go yet. Missing my wedding was the worst thing about this whole ordeal. Tell me what the church looked like. How many people came?"

"This could wait until you're feeling better." Though Clara smiled, she clutched her husband's arm for support.

"No, I want to hear about it now," Stacey said.

Davey still snuggled against Stacey who held Doug's hand.

"The church was beautiful and so was the reception hall. It looked exactly as you envisioned it." Clara supplied some of the details.

Stacey listened with her eyes closed.

"Oh, honey," Clara said. "You can't even keep your eyes open."

The tiredness in her own voice surprised Stacey. "I'm imagining what it looked like while you're telling me. Please go on."

Her father continued the remembrance. "Everyone you invited came, and possibly a few extras. Of course, they were all upset when you couldn't be located. Many stayed to pray with us."

Stacey opened her eyes. "I'll have to thank them all. The prayers helped, I know. What did you do with all the food?"

"Since so many of the guests stayed at the church waiting for news about you, we invited them all to eat. What was left, we sent to the homeless shelter."

"Good idea." The pain medicine she'd been given made her brain feel fuzzy. She yawned.

"I think it's time for us to go," Clara said.

Stacey didn't argue this time. Her mother and father kissed her goodbye. She gave Davey one last kiss and a hug. She clung to Doug's hand as her family left. "Stay with me just a little longer."

"I'll stay all night if you want. I can sleep right here in the chair."

"I'd like that. It's unnerving to know that horrible man who kidnapped me is right here in this hospital."

Doug grinned. "You don't have to worry about him. Four more FBI agents arrived while you were being examined. They aren't going to let him get away."

Stacey frowned. "I don't understand why they didn't come sooner. Wouldn't I have been found faster if more FBI men had been here?"

"Agent Benedict is new on the job. His colleagues probably didn't think he was on the right track when he came here after you disappeared. You didn't fit the profile of the other missing women. Now that they're all convinced the suspect is the one responsible for the others, they're going to see if they can get any information out of him about their locations. They'll be looking for his personal vehicle, too. It should be fairly close. I suspect he stole that Falcon to transport you to wherever his own car or van is located. He knew he couldn't leave town right away because so many police were canvassing the area. So, he hid out, waiting for it to get dark before he carried you to who knows where."

Though Stacey could hear his words, not much made sense. No matter, she could learn more in the morning. No doubt the FBI agents would be questioning her then too. She yawned again.

Doug leaned over and kissed her. She felt safe and loved, but fell asleep before she could kiss him back.

■

It was almost three a.m. when Felix Zachary finally climbed into bed beside his wife. The phone rang. He grabbed it quickly, hoping to catch it before it woke Wendy. He wasn't successful.

She raised up on one elbow, her blond hair falling to the side, a slight frown marring her pretty face. "Who is it? What time is it?"

He didn't answer either of her questions. "Zachary here."

A dispatcher's voice, without a hint of emotion stated, "We need you back at the station. A.S.A.P.," and hung up.

Felix switched on the light and squinted at the clock. He'd worked nearly four additional hours of overtime because of all the clean-up and paperwork associated with the shooting of Stacey Wilbur's kidnapper. He sighed, sat up and hung his feet over the side of the bed.

"What is it?" Wendy asked.

He turned, leaned down and kissed her. "I don't know. Something's up. I have to go back in."

"You don't think it's about Stacey, do you?"

"No. Last I heard she was safe in the hospital. Doug's there with her."

"Good. I'm sorry you have to go back." She snuggled back into her pillow.

"Me too. I was looking forward to a nice peaceful Sunday."

After he had his uniform on, he bent to give Wendy a goodbye kiss, but she was already asleep. Lucky woman.

He arrived at the station to see a couple of the daytime men had been called in too.

"What's going on?" he asked the first one.

"Sounds like the new guy is in some trouble."

"New guy? You mean Aragon?"

"Yes. They say he's barricaded in his motel room with his gun. He's threatening to kill himself if anyone shows up. The chief wants to talk to you before anyone does anything."

Felix sprinted down the hall to the chief's office. If Aragon planned to kill himself, someone better get over there in a hurry and talk him out of it. The door stood open, but Felix knocked. "You wanted to see me?"

"Yes, Zachary. You've heard what's going on?"

"No details, just something about Aragon wanting to kill himself. Has anyone gone to talk to him?"

"Not yet. He's barricaded in his motel room and says if any officers respond he'll blow his brains out."

"Sounds like he's planning to do it either way."

"That's why I called you in. You've spent more time with him than anyone."

"You're probably right. Wilbur would be the second person."

"Yes, I thought of her because she's so good at talking people down in volatile situations, but she's in the hospital. Do you have any idea what might have triggered this response from Aragon? Did anything unusual occur when you two arrested Wilbur's kidnapper?"

Felix considered for a moment. Everything had happened so fast when they were chasing the suspect. At the time, neither he nor Aragon really knew who the man was. Aragon went after him first, gun in hand. Although Aragon had the suspect in his sights, he hadn't fired. Felix was the one who brought the man down and handled the arrest.

Now that he thought about it, Aragon had been unusually quiet, especially for a cop who always had an opinion on everything. What was eating him? Had to be something big.

"Want me to go over there and see if he'll talk to me?"

"That's the idea. See if you can find out what his problem is. Sergeant Navarro is already there. He's got a couple of our guys making sure everyone is out of the motel. We don't want any civilians getting hurt."

"Has the sergeant made contact with him?"

"Yeah, he called his room, but he hasn't made much headway."

"I'll go there now." Felix headed back to the parking lot, trying to think of how he might reach Aragon.

■

Felix parked the police car he'd driven to the motel down the street where it couldn't be seen from the motel room's window. He doubted that would be a problem anyway because the fog had rolled in with a vengeance. He didn't see the other two police cars with men in them, also parked on the street until he came next to them.

Aragon's black-and-yellow Mini Cooper was parked in the nearly empty lot in front of a room near the middle of the building. An older, one story structure, the motel was built in an "L" shape. The bottom of the "L" housed the motel office. Light from the office spilled out on an unmarked car parked in front of the entrance. Felix circled around, staying in the shadows until he reached the sedan. Obviously, Sergeant Navarro watched his approach, because the passenger door swung open.

"Glad you could make it, Zachary. Get in."

Felix slid in beside the sergeant. "What's going on? I know Aragon has threatened to kill himself, but he must be having second thoughts, or he wouldn't have let anyone know."

"My feeling exactly. The chief wanted to call in a SWAT team from Ventura, but frankly, I think seeing SWAT guys would cause him to pull the trigger right then and there. I'm hoping we can talk him out of it. I've made contact with him, but he's not willing to say much to me. What do you know about the guy?"

Felix shrugged. "He's not happy. Said he was disappointed that things were so dull in Rocky Bluff, but I don't think that was the truth. I think he liked the quiet. It got pretty intense tonight. He had the bead on the bad guy, but he didn't pull the trigger. I think he might have a serious problem he didn't bother to tell anyone about. Reminds me of the way I acted after I shot that unarmed man."

Abel held out his cell phone. "I've got the motel room phone on speed dial. Why don't you talk to him? See what he has to say."

"I'll use my own phone. Aragon gave me his cell number, I'll call it." It rang several times before Aragon answered. When he picked up, he definitely sounded like he'd been drinking.

"What'cha want?" His words ran together.

"It's me, Zachary. I want to know what you're up to, man."

"Why aren't you home with your wife? If I had a wife I'd be home with her, but I don't have a wife anymore."

"Is that what's bothering you? That your wife left you?"

"No way. Got no use for her. She took just about everything I had."

"What's the matter then?"

"You know."

"No, I don't know."

"You were there. You saw."

"What? What did I see?"

"If you don't know, I'm not telling." The connection ended.

Felix turned to Navarro. "He hung up."

"Did he say anything that might help us?"

Felix thought again about what happened earlier with the capture of Stacey's kidnapper. "Tonight, after I shot the suspect, Aragon was really quiet. Something happened, but I'm not sure what."

"Wait a couple of minutes, then call him back."

Felix redialed. Aragon answered quicker. "Hey, is that you, Zachary?"

"Yes, it is. Do you have something you want to say to me?"

"Want to know something."

"What's that?"

"How's Wilbur? Is she really okay? I like her, she's got a lot of guts for such a little gal."

Felix didn't know much about Stacey's condition except she was alive and in the hospital, but he figured it best to tell the truth. "All I know is she escaped from her kidnapper and Doug went and picked her up. I heard she had some kind of head trauma and she's in the hospital."

"Aw, man." Aragon sounded anguished. "I need to know how she is."

"I'll see what I can find out."

"Uh uh, you could tell me anything. How would I know if it's true or not?"

"I wouldn't lie to you. What good would that do?"

"Might keep me from killing myself."

Felix wasn't sure what Aragon was getting at. "What is it you want me to do?"

"I want to know Wilbur is okay. If she isn't and I didn't kill that bastard when I had the chance then I don't deserve to live." Aragon's voice broke.

"No, no, you're wrong. The FBI is glad he's alive. He's the only one who can tell them what happened to all those other women, if he's the one who took them."

"I don't care about anyone except Wilbur. We know who kidnapped her. I gotta find out for sure that she's all right." It sounded as though Aragon was crying.

"Okay, Aragon. I'll see what I can do. Stay cool. Don't do anything until you hear from me again." Felix hung up.

He turned to Navarro. "This is crazy. He wants to make sure Stacey is all right."

"We can call the hospital, find out how she's doing."

"That won't be enough for him. I think I might have this figured out."

Navarro frowned. "What do you mean?"

"He froze out there. He had a perfect shot to take out our suspect, but he didn't take it. Everything happened so fast, I didn't think anything about it at the time. I came on the scene after Aragon. I'm the one who shot the suspect. He should have done it, but he didn't. He's feeling guilty. I'm sure there's a lot more to it, but right now whatever's going on is all mixed up with Stacey's well-being. I think we're going to have to get her to come out here and let him see her for himself."

"The hospital isn't going to release her, and I don't think Doug will let her leave either."

"Aragon is going to shoot himself if we don't do something, and I think it's going to have to be quick. He's pretty emotional."

"Maybe she could call him."

Felix was already dialing the hospital. When the operator answered, he said, "Connect me with Stacey Wilbur's room, please."

"I can't do that. You'll have to call during daylight hours."

"I know it's late, but this is Officer Felix Zachary, Rocky Bluff P.D. It's a matter of life or death."

The operator said, "I'll connect you with the night supervisor on that floor."

Felix told Navarro what was happening.

A woman came on the line. "Nurse Spencer. How may I help you?"

"This is Officer Zachary, RBPD. It's imperative that I speak with Stacey Wilbur."

"That's impossible, Officer. She's on medication and she's asleep."

It was obvious he wasn't going to convince the woman of the seriousness of the situation. "Look, could you peek in the room and see if Detective Milligan is in there?"

"I don't need to look, I know he's there. Do you want me to give him a message?"

"Yes, please. Tell him to turn on his cell phone. That Officer Navarro must speak to him."

"We don't allow cell phones in the hospital."

"I know that, Nurse Spencer, but it's crucial that I speak with Detective Milligan. A man's life depends upon it."

"If it's that important, I suppose..."

"It's that important."

Felix could hear the sound of squeaky soles on a tile floor fading away into the distance. In a few moments she returned and came back on the line.

"He's got his phone on. I warned him to talk softly so he won't disturb the patient."

"Thank you." He pushed the button to end that connection, then quickly punched in Milligan's cell phone number.

The detective answered in a low voice, "What's up?"

"We've got a situation."

"What kind of situation?"

"Officer Aragon is threatening to commit suicide."

Milligan's voice rose two notches. "What? The new guy? What's his problem? What do you think I can do about it?"

"He wants to make sure Stacey is okay."

"Tell him she's resting peacefully. She has a concussion, but everything seems to be all right."

"That isn't going to be enough for him."

Milligan hollered, "What do you mean that isn't going to be enough for him?"

"He needs to see Stacey."

He was still shouting. "That isn't going to happen, Zachary."

Felix could hear another voice. A female voice. It sounded like Stacey.

"What's going on, Doug?"

■

CHAPTER 22

STACEY WAS HAVING a pleasant dream about walking down the aisle of the Rocky Bluff Community Church in her beautiful wedding dress. In the dream, Doug stood on the platform by the preacher, shouting something she couldn't understand. The shouting brought her out of her groggy sleep.

She opened her eyes and focused on Doug. He paced the floor, his cell phone against his ear.

"What...what's going on, Doug?" Her tongue felt fuzzy and she had trouble forming the words.

He whirled around to face her and his voice softened. "Go back to sleep, Stacey. This doesn't concern you."

He turned away from her and lowered his voice. "No way. She's in this hospital for a reason. She's not going anywhere and that's the end of it." He snapped the phone closed and slipped it in the pocket of his slacks.

He smoothed the hair back from her forehead. "It's all right, sweetheart. Shut your eyes."

She raised up on one elbow. Her head still hurt but not quite as much as it had earlier. "Who called?"

"Nothing for you to worry about."

She could tell Doug fought to appear calm, but he was agitated by whatever he'd been told. A deep crease marred his forehead.

"You were talking about me. Why?"

"You've been through too much already. Right now all you have to do is rest and get well."

Stacey's head throbbed with a dull ache. However, going back to sleep wasn't an option until Doug told her what was going on. "Whatever it is has something to do with me."

"No."

"Don't lie to me, Doug."

"You've got a concussion, remember?"

With the way her head ached, how could she forget? But it didn't matter, something was going on, something to do with her. "Tell me. I'm not giving up until you do. There's no way I can go back to sleep while wondering what that call was about."

Doug dropped into the chair next to the bed and took her hand. "That new guy, Aragon, is in some kind of trouble."

"What?"

Doug sighed, raised his eyebrows and stared at the ceiling.

Though still a bit fuzzy around the edges, her brain seemed to be working better now. "Spit it out or I'll call the station myself to find out."

"Okay, okay. Aragon is threatening to kill himself."

Horrified, Stacey squeezed Doug's hand. "Why?"

"I don't think anyone knows for sure, but he wants to know if you're okay."

Stacey considered what he said. "Telling him isn't enough. He has to see me." She let go of Doug, threw back the covers and hung her legs over the bed. "Where are my clothes?"

"Forget it, Stacey, you aren't going anywhere."

"Oh, yes I am. Look in the closet. See if my clothes are there."

He crossed his arms. "No. I'm not going to do it."

"Then I'll look for myself." The minute she tried to stand, she felt woozy and sat back down.

"See. You aren't in any condition to go anywhere."

She paused for a moment until her head cleared. She stood again, this time feeling more steady.

"I'm not going to give you your clothes."

"Then I'll just go like this." She started toward the door, feeling the cold air hitting her bare buttocks.

He grasped her arms. "Man, you are so stubborn. Let me talk to the nurse. I'll tell her what's going on, that a man's life is at stake and see what she says about you leaving."

"No, Doug. She can't let me, it's against hospital rules. What floor are we on?"

"The second. But get that idea out of your head. You can't go down stairs in your condition."

"What do you mean, my condition? I got hit on the head. My legs work fine." To be honest, they actually felt a bit rubbery, but she could tell she was wearing him down.

"You aren't going to give up, are you?"

"No, I'm not."

He shook his head, but went to the closet and pulled out a plastic bag and handed it to her. "Your clothes."

Dropping the bag at the end of the bed, she reached in and yanked out her panties and stepped into them. Then she slid her running shorts on.

She shrugged out of the hospital gown letting it drop into a puddle on the floor.

Doug's eyes grew huge. His cheeks flushed.

Someone's life was in danger; she didn't have time to worry about modesty. She fastened her bra and pulled the T-shirt over her head. She jammed her feet into her running shoes.

Doug stared at her. He seemed stunned.

"Come on. There's no time to waste." She grabbed Doug's hand, poked her head out the door, saw the sign for the stairs and pulled him after her.

Her head hurt with every step she took, reminding her why she was in the hospital. A couple of times she had to pause and lean against the wall.

"This is crazy," Doug said. "Let me help you back to your room."

"No. I could never live with myself if Aragon killed himself. I have to at least try to talk him out of it. He wants to see me. You'll feel bad too, if you don't help me."

"When you put it that way, I don't want the guy to die either." Doug opened the heavy exit door to the stairs.

Stacey took two steps down. She felt light-headed and had to grab the railing with both hands to keep from collapsing.

Doug scooped her into his arms and carried her to the bottom of the staircase. He turned and used his backside to push against the exit bar. Though the parking lot was full as usual, no one seemed to be around to notice their unorthodox departure.

"Where's your car?" Stacey asked.

"Same place I parked it when I brought you in here, by the front entrance in the 'no parking' zone."

"Good thinking. Hurry."

He set her down by the passenger side, pulled the door open and helped her inside. "We shouldn't be doing this. You ought to be back inside the hospital sleeping."

"They kept waking me up to make sure I was okay. I'm proving it now."

Closing the door, he said, "Put your seat belt on."

Once he was settled in the driver's seat and started the car, she asked, "Where are we going?"

He pounded the steering wheel. "I have no idea. I didn't ask."

"Give me your cell phone."

He shook his head, but reached in his pocket for his cell and tossed it to her.

While he backed out of the parking lot, she made the call.

Zachary answered. "I hope you've reconsidered, Milligan."

"This is Stacey. We're on our way. Where's Vaughn?"

"Oh, Stacey, thank you. Do you know that old motel at the far end of Valley Boulevard? It's about four blocks north of the furniture store."

She knew exactly where it was. It was often frequented by prostitutes and other unsavory characters. She'd gone there a few times looking for people to interview in her position as a vice investigator. Weird place for a cop to be. "Yeah, I know it. What's he doing there?"

"That's where he lives."

"No wonder he's depressed."

"It's more than that, Wilbur. I'm glad you're coming. If you don't show up to prove you're okay, I'm sure we'll lose him. For some reason he feels guilty about what happened to you. Not sure what that's all about."

"Tell him I'll be there soon."

"I'll do that. Thank you. I think we're the only two who knew this guy."

"Obviously, we didn't know him enough." She closed the phone.

■

Besides the sergeant and Zachary, Aragon knew other cops had to be waiting near the motel. He ought to end it now and everyone could go home. No way could a happy ending come from this. If he didn't kill himself, he'd be sent to a psychiatric hospital or stuck with regular psychiatric visits. With his life in law enforcement ended, he had nothing to live for.

The one thing that kept him from putting his service revolver in his mouth and pulling the trigger was seeing Stacey Wilbur and knowing she was okay. She was the one person who accepted him when he came to work for Rocky Bluff P.D. She respected him and his abilities.

Oh, Zachary was nice enough, but he was all caught up in his marriage and the baby on its way.

He couldn't accept anyone's report on Stacey's condition. Cops lied all the time to get what they wanted. It was his fault the guy who grabbed Stacey wasn't in the morgue. If she was there instead, he had no desire to go on.

If Stacey did come, what then?

He didn't know. Life wasn't worth living. He'd definitely found that out. After all his work, he had nothing to show for it. No wife, no home, and now, no job.

He'd decide what to do after he saw Stacey. He ran his fingers over his service revolver.

■

Doug drove slowly. After all, he didn't want to do anything reckless or run over any bumps that might cause Stacey any discomfort. Only remnants of fog still swirled around so he couldn't blame his reluctance to travel faster on lack of visibility.

She glanced at the speedometer. "Can't you go any faster?"

"I'm going the speed limit."

She sighed and stared out the window.

As they headed down Valley Boulevard, she said, "Slow down when you go by the furniture store. I'd love to see the angel."

"It's gone."

She frowned. "What do you mean?"

"Your kidnapper's car crashed into it. The angel is nothing more than a pile of shattered glass."

A wave of disappointment flowed over her. "Darn. I really wanted to see it."

"The crowd in front of the window made the kidnapper slow down."

"Maybe that was the whole reason the angel was here. Otherwise, he might have gotten away." She smiled.

"Maybe." Such a concept wasn't anything Doug could put his brain around. If that's what Stacey wanted to think, that was fine with him.

They rode in silence for a few more minutes until they neared the furniture store. A blue-and-white police car sat in front and crime scene tape fluttered across the gaping hole. A uniformed police officer and a man in civilian clothes stood near the alley.

"Is that where the suspect was shot?" Stacey asked.

"From what I heard, yes."

Putting her head back, she closed her eyes for the remainder of the drive.

Though no emergency lights flashed, Doug spotted two police cars parked far enough away from the motel that they couldn't be seen by Aragon. An unmarked sedan was near a blinking No Vacancy sign by the motel's office. Doug maneuvered his car beside it.

"Stay put, Stacey, until I find out what the plan is." He climbed out of the car without waiting for her.

Felix Zachary and Abel Navarro joined him.

"How's Stacey?" Navarro asked.

Without a thought, he said, "Stubborn."

Felix laughed. "I think the sergeant meant her physical condition."

"I know. She ought to be in the hospital, but the second she heard about Aragon, nothing I said could stop her. She dressed and we sneaked out of the hospital by way of the stairs."

"Sounds like our Stacey," Abel said.

"So what's the plan?" Doug wasn't thrilled with the idea of the woman he loved confronting Aragon. No one knew enough about him. Maybe he wanted to do her harm.

"Zachary will call him and tell him she's here. Maybe all she'll have to do is step out of the car so he can see her."

"That better be all." Doug heard a car door slam and knew Stacey was done waiting.

Standing on the other side of the vehicle, she hollered, "Which room is Vaughn's?"

Doug frowned. Vaughn? He'd never even heard anyone say Aragon's first name before. Stacey must've known him better than Doug realized.

"The only room with the light on," Abel said. "That's his car in front."

A sliver of light escaped where drapes didn't quite meet in a room near the center of the motel. Stacey walked in that direction.

"Stacey, for crying out loud..." Doug started after her.

Abel caught him by the arm. "No, you stay here. Zachary, call Aragon and let him know Wilbur is on her way to his room."

"Who knows what he might do?" Doug turned to Abel. "You told me yourself the man was emotionally unbalanced."

Zachary signaled for quiet. He held his cell phone to his ear. "Open up, Aragon. Stacey's right outside."

The door opened a crack, then halfway. Doug caught a brief glimpse of Aragon in a white T-shirt and what looked like uniform trousers.

Stacey reached the door. Doug heard her say, "Hi, Vaughn. See, I'm okay."

"That's far enough," Doug hollered.

Abel clutched Doug's arm tighter. "Knock it off. Stacey knows what she's doing."

Stacey didn't act like she'd heard him anyway. Oh, Lord, she stepped inside the room and shut the door behind her.

"We've got to go after her. No telling what that maniac will do to her."

"He isn't going to hurt her," Zachary said.

"You don't know that. The guy was planning to kill himself, who's to say he won't take her with him." Doug could hardly think. Only a few hours ago he'd thought he'd lost her. Then he had her back, and now her life was in jeopardy again. He wrenched his arm away from Abel's grasp.

Stepping in front of Doug, Abel said, "Stop right now, Milligan. Control yourself or I'll call one of the officers to escort you from the scene. She'll be fine. She's a master at calming situations, you know that."

Doug's stomach churned. Bile rose in his throat. "I should have been the one to go in and talk to him."

"Oh sure. He hardly knows you. What do you think you could have done that Zachary hasn't already tried? He's spent time with Aragon since he came on the job."

Doug didn't answer. He strode toward the end of the parking lot and back again. If something happened to Stacey now how could he ever explain it to her son or her parents?

Time passed slowly. Dawn approached. The sky lightened. Pewter turned to blue.

Doug rejoined the other men. "How much longer are we going to wait?"

"As long as it takes," Abel said.

■

CHAPTER 23

THE FIRST THING Stacey noticed when she entered the room was the gun Vaughn Aragon gripped tightly in his hand.

He only opened the door wide enough for her to step inside before closing it again. "I'm glad to see you. I didn't know if they were telling me the truth." The circles under his eyes had darkened. "I had to know if you are really okay."

"I'm still a bit shaky. Have a big knot on my head." She pulled aside her hair to show him.

"Nasty bump." Aragon pulled out the chair that faced a small table serving as a desk. "Please, Wilbur, sit down."

"Why don't you call me Stacey? Is it okay if I call you Vaughn?" She sat.

"Yeah, sure."

"Why don't you tell me what's going on here, Vaughn? I'm a good listener."

"No, that's not necessary. I just wanted to make sure you were all right. I thought maybe they were just saying so to keep me from... well, you know." The last part he spoke so quietly she had to strain to hear him.

Stacey shrugged. "I sneaked out of the hospital to come here. I'm probably going to catch all kinds of grief because of it, so you might as well make it worth my while." If he only wanted to see her, then he wouldn't have let her in the room.

"I don't know what to say." He still had a tight grip on his gun.

"I like you. You're a good police officer. You've already proven that."

Vaughn sat on the end of the bed across from her. He shook his head. "No, what I proved tonight is I'm not fit to be a policeman."

"What makes you say such a thing?" She really couldn't understand what was going on with him.

"I was the one closest to that bastard that grabbed you. He was right in front of me and I had a perfect shot. I just couldn't pull the trigger." Tears filled his eyes.

"Why not?"

"I froze." He didn't say anything more for several moments, when he did, his lower lip trembled. "I'm not fit for police work anymore."

"I don't believe that."

Vaughn put his head in his hands, the side of the gun pressed against his temple, barrel aimed at the ceiling. "That's part of the reason I left LAPD. It's why I came to this department, the smallest I could find with an opening."

"Tell me what happened to make you feel this way."

"Oh, I told the department shrink, but she didn't help any. I gave her all the answers I knew she wanted to hear. She bought what I said told me and my bosses I was fit to go back to work. I thought once I was back on the street, I'd be kept busy enough I wouldn't think about it. But the nightmares didn't stop."

Stacey reached out and touched his shoulder. "I'm not a shrink, but as a fellow officer and friend, I want to help. What started all this?"

Suicides among law enforcement officers rank among the highest of all professions. Stacey prayed that Vaughn wouldn't carry through on his threat—whether she was in the room or not. It was obvious he needed help, help she wasn't qualified to give. Hopefully, talking through whatever demonized him could deescalate the situation enough for him to put away the gun.

"I shot a kid."

"Oh, dear." She waited for more.

"I didn't know he was a kid. He was robbing a mom-and-pop store and when I arrived on the scene, he started shooting at me, so I shot back." Vaughn's knee began shaking.

"Sounds justified."

"Yeah, that's what everyone says."

"What happened after that?" Stacey shifted in her chair. The headache worsened.

"Do you know how it feels to be questioned by your supervisors like you're a suspect?"

"Is that what they did?"

He nodded. "Right after it happened, yeah. They said it was a mandatory debriefing. Then they made me give a urine and blood sample."

She grimaced, partly because of what he said and partly because of the pain in her head.

"They told me I had the right to have a lawyer present. What for? I didn't do anything wrong. At least that's what they kept telling me, but they kept on with the interrogation."

"I'm so sorry." She wanted him to keep talking.

"I couldn't sleep. I had terrible nightmares. I'm still having them. I'd start crying for no reason. My wife, my dear, loyal, concerned wife, thought I was going nuts. She filed for divorce and got nearly everything I'd worked for."

"How sad." She longed to be back in the hospital and get something for her headache, but she couldn't leave until she knew Vaughn would be okay.

"I really thought I would get better working here."

"You sure came through for me when I needed you." She touched his shoulder again.

He gave her an ironic smile. "There weren't any guns involved with that guy."

"You know you aren't the only one who has gone through something like this."

"That's what they say." His glum expression returned.

"Killing someone, no matter the circumstances, is certainly going to have a big effect on anyone with a conscience. Thank God, I've never had that experience, but I know someone who has. You know him too. He shot an unarmed suspect. Of course, at the time he thought the guy was armed."

Vaughn turned toward her, frowning. "You're just saying that."

She smiled. "It's someone you've been working with quite regularly." She could tell she'd caught his interest.

"Who are you talking about? Surely not Butler. I can't imagine that guy shooting anyone."

Her head throbbed even more, making it difficult to think. "No, not Butler. I'm talking about Felix Zachary. I don't know all the details, but he had a difficult time after he shot that guy." She touched the knot on the back of her head hoping to make the pain subside. Didn't work.

"I wish he'd said something."

"Why would he? Did you tell him anything about your situation?"

"No." For the first time he released his grip on the gun and put it beside him on the bed.

"I think you should let Felix come in and talk to you."

She could tell Vaughn was mulling around the idea. "My head is giving me fits. I need to get back to the hospital. Let me ask Felix to come and talk to you."

"He won't want to. By now he probably thinks I'm dangerous."

Stacey shrugged, stood and held out her hand. "Why don't you give me your gun? Then he'll know it's safe to come in."

Vaughn's reluctance was apparent in his expression. He stared at the gun for a moment. In a quick motion, he picked it up.

Stacey feared he was going to shoot himself despite their long talk. Instead he handed the gun to her.

She relaxed a bit, though the pain in her head didn't. "Thank you, Vaughn. You've done the right thing. I'll just get Felix and you can talk to him. We'll all work together on this. I mean it."

Though she felt dizzy and wasn't seeing clearly, she walked to the door and opened it, gun in hand. "Felix," she called out hoping the others were close enough to hear her, "Aragon wants to talk to you."

She stepped out, shocked by bright sunlight. She shaded her eyes with her hand. The edges of her vision blurred. Everything dimmed. She felt weak. Her legs became rubbery. Dizzy, she fought to stay conscious, but lost. Blackness crept over her and she welcomed it.

CHAPTER 24

WHEN THE DOOR opened and Stacey came out, Doug hollered, "Thank God, she's all right."

Abel stated matter-of-factly, "She's got a gun in her hand. Must be Aragon's."

She swayed on her feet.

Doug darted toward her. "Stacey, what's wrong?"

Aragon came out of the darkened doorway and caught Stacey before she crumpled to the sidewalk. The gun fell from her hand and bounced once on the cement. All three of the waiting police officers ducked instinctively, though Doug only paused momentarily before continuing to run toward her.

He shouted, "What did you do to her?" He couldn't think. Crazy emotions bombarded him. He should have never let her go into that room. He almost lost her once. Surely it couldn't be happening again.

Felix Zachary caught up with him and grabbed his arm. "He didn't do anything, man. She passed out, he caught her."

Doug realized Felix was right. He pulled away from Felix and moved to Aragon, who held a limp Stacey under the arms. "I'll take her."

Zachary reached down, scooped up the service revolver, and passed it to Sergeant Navarro who had joined them.

Doug gathered Stacey into his arms and put his lips close to her ear. "Stacey, can you hear me?"

Her eyelids fluttered, lifted, and she stared at him. "Doug? What happened?"

"You came out of Aragon's room and collapsed."

She rubbed her eyes. "Put me down. I have something to say."

"Not until we get to the car. I'm taking you right back to the hospital." Doug turned and started to walk away with her.

She struggled against him. "No, no, not yet. I have something important to tell Felix."

Zachary stepped closer to Stacey. "I'm here."

"All of you have to hear this. You too, Vaughn."

The three men gathered around Stacey still in Doug's arms.

Doug couldn't help glaring at them. Nothing was as important as Stacey's well-being. He was scared for her. "Whatever it is, tell them quickly. We're going back to the hospital. I'm not taking anymore chances with you."

"Felix, you're the one who needs to talk to Vaughn. He'll listen to you."

"Well, sure. If that's what you want." Zachary glanced from Stacey to Aragon.

"I know you can relate to what he's going through. Vaughn's problem is the same as the one you had," Stacey said, her voice weak.

Zachary's dark eyebrows nearly came together. "You shot an unarmed suspect?"

"He was armed," Aragon said, "but he was just a kid. I don't see how talking to you will change anything."

"Give me a chance, Aragon. The suspect I killed was a young guy too. I can't fix your problem, but I might be able to help you come to grips with it. I do understand what you're going through." Zachary turned back toward Sergeant Navarro. He nodded.

Aragon stepped back inside his room, Zachary followed.

Stacey smiled. "Now you can take me back to the hospital."

■

Doug and Stacey entered through the front door of the hospital. After a short explanation, the nurse on duty raised her thinly plucked eyebrows and shook her head, but she didn't bother to scold. Instead she brought a wheelchair and pushed it under Stacey. Turning to Doug, she said, "You may do the honors."

When the doors of the elevator opened on the second floor, the nurse on duty was the same paragon of patient care who'd been there when Stacey sneaked out. With eyes glaring, she came out from behind the nurses' station and unleashed her wrath.

She shook a knobby finger in Stacey's face. "Being a police officer does not grant you special privileges around here, young lady. How do you expect to recover from your injuries when you don't obey doctor's orders?"

Stacey smiled. Doug pushed her toward her room.

The nurse trotted alongside the wheelchair. "I've reported your absence to the doctor. We'll see what he has to say about this."

"Give her a break." Doug frowned at the nurse. "She already has a headache and you're making it worse."

The nurse's pants made a swishing sound as she hurried to keep up with him. "Your girlfriend should have thought about her head before she snuck out of here in the middle of the night."

Stacey propped an elbow on the armrest of the chair and held her pounding head. All she wanted to do was curl up in bed and go to sleep. She thought about Vaughn and wondered if Felix could get through to him. She'd done all she could. Whatever happened next was out of her hands. Now it was time to think about herself.

Though the nurse tried to elbow her way past Doug to help Stacey into bed, he blocked her attempt. With gentleness Stacey appreciated, he lifted her onto the sheet and pulled the blankets up. He leaned down and kissed her. "Is there anything else I can do for you?"

She gazed up at his handsome face, his dimple hidden by anxiety, stubble on his cheeks and chin, his good suit rumpled. Despite her throbbing head, she felt safe and loved. "When can we get married?"

"As soon as you're out of this hospital."

The nurse huffed, rolled her eyes and stomped out of the room.

Doug snuggled down beside Stacey and cradled her in his arms. His lips on hers was the last thing she remembered before she drifted off to sleep.

■

After a few hours, Stacey woke headache free. In mid-afternoon, the doctor allowed her to check out of the hospital with orders not to exert herself.

When she and Doug were in the car, she said, "Tell me about Vaughn Aragon. Have you heard what happened after we left?"

"Yes, he's agreed to psychiatric counseling. He went through something like that when he was with LAPD, but he wasn't honest with the psychiatrist and only told her what he thought she wanted to hear. He must've been convincing since they took him back."

"He told me that too. Will he be reinstated to our department?"

Doug shrugged. "I suspect it'll depend upon how the counseling goes. Zachary sounded positive about what might happen. He's going to keep an eye on Aragon, and make sure he does what he's supposed to." He grinned, his dimple deepened. "I have other news."

"What?" She wasn't sure what to expect, but hoped it was something good.

"The FBI agents found your engagement ring in the suspect's pants' pocket. Unfortunately, they're hanging onto it as evidence."

"I'm so glad they found it. No telling how long it'll be before I get it back, but at least I know that it'll be back on my finger one of these days. Have they learned anything from him?"

"They haven't said much to me or anyone else. What I do know is the FBI believes they got the right guy. And, they still want to talk to you but said they could wait until Monday."

"I don't have a whole lot to tell them. Most of the time I was unconscious in the back of that strange van."

Stacey was anxious to get home, but instead she realized Doug drove toward his Victorian.

"Why are we going to your house? I really want to go home and see Davey and my folks."

Doug smiled but didn't change direction.

When he pulled up in front of his house, he said, "You are home."

"I don't understand."

"Come inside and you will." He winked and took her hand, led her up the walk and into the screened porch. She blinked in surprise. Davey's bike and some of his trucks and other toys were in the corner. "What's going on?"

"It'll all be clear in a moment."

He opened the front door. Her mother and father jumped up from Doug's couch, big grins on their faces. "Finally, you're here," her mother said, moving toward her with arms outstretched.

Davey came running from the direction of the kitchen and threw himself at her. "Mommy, you're back."

She didn't feel strong enough to pick him up, but leaned down to hug him tight. She brushed his hair back with her hand and kissed his forehead. Her mother and father surrounded them both, telling her how much they loved her.

When Stacey stood up and looked around she saw Reverend Cookmeyer standing in front of the French doors. He smiled, his teeth as white as his hair. He stepped forward. "If you're up to it, we thought we might have a wedding this afternoon."

She gaped at Doug, then her parents. She frowned. "This is a nice idea, but I really wanted to wear my wedding dress..."

Clara came toward her. "Then I guess you'd better go upstairs and put it on. Let's go up and I'll help you."

Somewhat overwhelmed, Stacey couldn't quite comprehend what was happening.

Gordon Butler stepped out of the kitchen. "While you were in the hospital, some of the guys helped us move my stuff to your folks' place, and most of yours and Davey's stuff over here. Hope that's okay with you."

Doug moved closer to her. "You and Davey are living here now. All that's left to do is tie the knot."

"Wow. Thank you, Gordon." She still had trouble putting her mind around what was taking place.

Gordon grinned. "My wedding present to both of you. Doug's been trying to get me out of his house for months."

"That's the truth." Doug had a bemused expression on his face.

"Thank you." She turned toward her mother. "I've been dreaming about wearing my dress for my wedding."

Her mother put her arm around Stacey. "Then we best get upstairs and get you into it."

■

Gordon had called the florist, retrieved the nosegay, and put it in Doug's refrigerator. Stacey carried it as she came to the first landing of the stairs barefooted, her father beside her. The high heels that went with the dress had been left behind in her bedroom at her parent's house, but it didn't matter.

Since she was still a bit wobbly, heels wouldn't have been a good idea.

A CD of the standard wedding processional began.

Though her hair was still damp from a quick shower, she felt beautiful in the light blue gossamer gown as it swirled around her knees. Doug's smile was huge. Tears glistened in his eyes as he gazed at her coming down the staircase.

He waited next to the minister. Gordon stood beside him wearing a goofy grin, her mother and Davey stood on the other side.

When Davey spotted her bare feet, he pointed and started giggling. "Mommy forgot her shoes."

Everyone joined in the laughter, and for the first time Stacey noticed the French doors were opened wide. Some of the police officers and their wives that had been invited to the first ceremony stood on the patio: Ryan and Barbara Strickland and their three sons, Felix and Wendy Zachary, Abel and Maria Navarro and their little girl, Doug's partner, Frank Marshall and his wife, Chief McKenzie and a tall man Stacey didn't recognize smiled broadly at her.

Stacey gasped. "Oh, my goodness, I can't believe you all came."

Doug grinned. "That tall guy in the back, that's FBI Agent Benedict. He helped organize the search for you."

Benedict raised his hand. "I wouldn't have missed this for the world. Most of my cases don't have happy endings."

Dipping her head, Stacey said, "Everyone, thank you. I know you all had a part in my rescue."

Reverend Cookmeyer cleared his throat. "Let's get on with the ceremony, shall we?"

Stacey and her father stepped in front of the minister who then asked, "Who gives this bride to the groom?"

Clyde took Stacey's hand and put it in Doug's. "Her mother, Davey, and I do."

Davey nodded his head and grinned. "Yep, we do." He gave two thumbs up.

"Let us pray," Reverend Cookmeyer said.

Stacey couldn't concentrate on his words, all that came through was something about being truly joined in the holy state of matrimony and finally, the Amen.

When she raised her head, the minister said, "I'm going to get right down to the business of getting you two married. Does anyone present have any objections?"

Stacey glanced at Doug. "Not me."

He added, "Or me."

Davey piped up with, "Me either."

Reverend Cookmeyer smiled. "That being the case, let's begin. We are gathered here today, before God and these witnesses, to see Doug Milligan and Stacey Wilbur joined together in holy matrimony. Doug, will you have this woman to be your wife? Will you promise your life to her in all love and honor, in all duty and service, in all faith and tenderness, to live with her, to cherish her, according to the ordinance of God, in the holy bond of marriage?"

Doug faced her. "I will."

The minister asked Stacey the same questions, and she quickly answered, "Yes, I will."

"Doug, will you please say these vows after me. I, Doug, take Stacey to be my wedded wife."

Doug repeated the words.

Reverend Cookmeyer said the next phrases and Doug repeated them. "And I do promise before God and these witnesses to be your loving and faithful husband in plenty and in want, in joy and in sorrow, and in sickness and in health, for as long as we both shall live."

The minister turned to Stacey who made the same promises. Her heart swelled with love and joy for the man who held her hands and gazed at her so lovingly. She hoped he could tell how much she loved him.

Gordon had to search in his pockets before he finally found the ring to give to the minister. He passed it to Doug who slipped it onto Stacey's finger. "I give you this ring as a token and pledge of our abiding love."

"Does someone have a ring for the groom?" Cookmeyer asked.

"I do. I do." Davey jumped up and down and waved his raised arm before giving the gold band to his mother. "Grandma said you're supposed to put this on Doug's finger."

"Thank you, Davey." Stacey could hardly hold back the tears that threatened as she slipped the band on Doug's finger and repeated what Doug had said to her.

"Before God and these witnesses, and by the authority vested in me as a minister of God's holy church and the state of California, I now declare you husband and wife. Whomever God has joined together, let no man put asunder. You may now kiss your bride."

Doug gathered Stacey into his arms and kissed her with love and passion.

Davey hugged their legs, making an effort to squeeze in between them. Her parents clapped. Gordon made a loud whooping noise. The guests on the patio cheered.

When Doug finally released her, Reverend Cookmeyer said, "May I introduce Mr. and Mrs. Douglas Milligan."

The guests flowed in from the patio. Hugs and kisses followed with congratulations and well-wishes. Her mother served sandwiches and salad, followed by slices from the top layer of the wedding cake she'd put aside from the day before.

"Oh, Mom, I can't believe you did that."

"I knew in my heart we'd get you back and when we did, the first thing you'd want to do was get married. What's a wedding without cake?"

After everyone had eaten and Reverend Cookmeyer and most of the guests left, Clara said, "Dad and I have one more surprise."

"What's that?"

"Davey's coming home with us tonight."

"Yep, Grandpa's going to play a new video game with me."

She knew it had to be some special game for Davey to be willing to be away from her, but she couldn't help but wonder if that meant that Gordon would still be here? Stacey glanced at him, and she guessed her thought was apparent in her expression.

Gordon's complexion brightened. "Don't worry, I'm going home with them too. You and Doug will have the house to yourself."

"Mrs. Milligan, what do you think about that?" Doug asked.

"Mr. Milligan, I think it's wonderful." They kissed again, much longer than the wedding kiss.

The ceremony wasn't anything like Stacey had dreamed, but in some ways, it was far better.

ABOUT THE AUTHOR

Award winning author F.M. Meredith, also known as Marilyn Meredith, is the author of nearly thirty published novels. Her latest in the Rocky Bluff P.D. crime series, from Oak Tree Press, is *Angel Lost*. F. M. has been neighbors with and has many relatives who are in law enforcement and for many years lived in a beach community with a strong resemblance to Rocky Bluff. Marilyn is a member of EPIC, four chapters of Sisters in Crime, including the Internet chapter, Mystery Writers of America, and on the board of the Public Safety Writers of America. Visit her at http://fictionforyou.com and her blog at http://marilynmeredith.blogspot.com

32463650R10120

Made in the USA
Charleston, SC
14 August 2014